What Man In [...]
Would Pass Up A Few Months
Alone With A Woman
Like Maggie?

The kind of man who knew that she deserved better—that she would expect it. To her, he was just another damaged human being she could fix.

But this wasn't about her. It was about him, and as much as he would have liked to deny it, he wanted his life back. If he did go, and failed, he'd be no worse off than he'd been before. With her help, he'd at least have a chance.

"If you say no, I'll have to reduce myself to kidnapping. You don't want me to commit a felony, do you?"

An honest-to-goodness chuckle rose in his chest and it felt...good. It had been a long time since anyone had made him feel this way. "You win. When do we leave?"

Dear Reader,

Why not make reading Silhouette Desire every month your New Year's resolution? It's a lot easier—and a heck of a lot more enjoyable—than diet or exercise!

We're starting 2006 off with a bang by launching a brand-new continuity: THE ELLIOTTS. The incomparable Leanne Banks gives us a glimpse into the lives of this high-powered Manhattan family, with *Billionaire's Proposition*. More stories about the Elliotts will follow every month throughout the year.

Also launching this month is Kathie DeNosky's trilogy, THE ILLEGITIMATE HEIRS. Three brothers born on the wrong side of the blanket learned they are destined for riches. The drama begins with *Engagement between Enemies*. *USA TODAY* bestselling author Annette Broadrick is back this month with *The Man Means Business*, a boss/secretary book with a tropical setting and a sensual story line.

Rounding out the month are great stories with heroes to suit your every mood. Roxanne St. Claire gives us a bad boy who needs to atone for *The Sins of His Past*. Michelle Celmer gives us a dedicated physical therapist who is not above making a few late-night *House Calls*. And Barbara Dunlop (who is new to Desire) brings us a sexy cowboy whose kiss is as shocking as a *Thunderbolt over Texas*.

Here's to keeping that New Year's resolution!

Melissa Jeglinski

Melissa Jeglinski
Senior Editor

Please address questions and book requests to:
Silhouette Reader Service
U.S.: 3010 Walden Ave., P.O. Box 1325, Buffalo, NY 14269
Canadian: P.O. Box 609, Fort Erie, Ont. L2A 5X3

MICHELLE CELMER

HOUSE CALLS

Silhouette® Desire

Published by Silhouette Books
America's Publisher of Contemporary Romance

SILHOUETTE BOOKS

ISBN 0-373-76703-X

HOUSE CALLS

Visit Silhouette Books at www.eHarlequin.com

Printed in U.S.A.

Books by Michelle Celmer

Silhouette Desire

Playing by the Baby Rules #1566
The Seduction Request #1626
Bedroom Secrets #1656
Round-the-Clock Temptation #1683
House Calls #1703

Silhouette Intimate Moments

Running on Empty #1342
Out of Sight #1398

MICHELLE CELMER

lives in southeastern Michigan with her husband, their three children, two dogs and two cats. When she's not writing or busy being a mom, you can find her in the garden or curled up with a romance novel. And if you twist her arm real hard you can usually persuade her into a day of power shopping.

Michelle loves to hear from readers. Visit her Web site at: www.michellecelmer.com, or write her at P.O. Box 300, Clawson, MI 48017.

To my children, who never fail to amaze, bewilder, confuse and delight me—and always make me proud.

One

At the sound of a car door slamming, Pete Morgan wheeled himself across the library to the window overlooking the circular drive, but he was too late to see the occupant of the dark blue SUV parked there.

What difference did it make? He'd only gone to the window out of habit. It wasn't as if he got many visitors these days. Or wanted any, for that matter.

The flowers and get-well cards had stopped arriving soon after he was released from the hospital, and after weeks of enduring the seemingly endless looks of pity from friends and colleagues, he'd begun turning visitors away. It had taken a few weeks, but people finally got the hint and stopped coming altogether. Now he spent his days alone in his private wing of the house. The solitude it provided suited him just fine.

He stared out the window, trying to recall when he'd last

been outside. The afternoon sun looked warm and inviting and a gentle breeze swayed the trees bordering the ten-acre estate. Occasionally he yearned to get out. He missed the sting of the sun on his back as he sliced across the lake on water skis, the burn of his muscles as he scaled the jagged face of a mountain, the wind in his hair as he biked the trails at Stony Creek State Park. Those had been the days he'd lived for, the days he'd felt truly free.

Those days were over.

He stared out the window, remembering all that he'd lost—all that he would never get back. When he heard the door open, it might have been five minutes later or it could have been an hour.

"Peter?" a voice said stiffly, as though the mere mention of his name caused enormous regret.

He didn't bother turning to face her. He knew what he would see if he did—disappointment, pity. He wasn't in the mood.

"What do you want, Mother?"

"Your father and I would like to have a word with you."

Glancing over his shoulder, he saw that his father stood next to her in the doorway—towered over her was more like it. Charles Morgan, a force to be reckoned with. There had been a time, long ago, when Pete had respected his father's powerful presence, feared it even. Not anymore. He'd grown immune to him a long time ago. "I'm afraid you'll have to call my secretary for an appointment. I'm booked solid this afternoon."

The pinched, irritated look he received from his father gave Pete tremendous satisfaction.

"I don't find your sarcasm amusing," he thundered. "You will apologize to your mother this instant."

"Or else what?" He swiveled to face them. "You'll ground me? You'll take away my driving privileges? News flash: I'm not going anywhere."

"I've had enough of your attitude." A vein pulsed at his father's temple. "You've spent weeks wallowing in self-pity when you should have been working to rehabilitate yourself."

"What you think is of no concern to me. If you insist that I stay here, you're just going to have to learn to live with me this way." Pete tossed the medical journal he'd been reading on the table next to the couch and spun back to the window. "Maybe I'm happy the way I am."

"Nonsense," his mother said, her voice softer but no less disapproving. "You're a doctor. You won't be satisfied until you've made a complete recovery."

"Has it occurred to either one of you that I may not make a complete recovery? Have you forgotten that my leg was nearly blown off?"

"Morgans are fighters," his father replied, as if his word was law. As if that reversed the damage Pete had sustained. Talk about arrogant.

"You'll learn to walk again," his father said. "Starting today."

He sensed his mother crossing the room, and in his peripheral vision saw her lift a hand to his shoulder, then pull away before she touched him. Touching had never been a big hit at the Morgan estate. His father had always believed in tough love. Affection hadn't factored into the program. Obviously that hadn't changed in the years he'd been away.

"Peter—" she said gently, before his father's voice boomed behind her.

"We're wasting our time here. He won't listen."

He sensed her pause, as though she might actually defy her husband and speak her mind for the first time in her life, but her hand dropped to her side and she backed away. Their retreating footsteps told him the conversation was over.

"Suppose I don't ever walk," he said aloud, wheeling back to the window. "What then?"

"Suppose you stop acting like a big baby and at least try."

The comment came from neither of his parents and Pete swung around, startled to find that he wasn't alone. "I beg your pardon?"

She stood across the room, her back to him, a compact little package of luscious curves and softness poured into a snug pair of blue jeans and a clingy red shirt. She gazed up at the bookcases spanning the north wall. "You know, I don't think I've ever seen so many books in one place." She laughed to herself. "I mean, I've obviously seen lots of books at the library and the bookstore, but not in someone's house. I wonder if they've all been read?"

She pulled a leather-bound copy of *The Hobbit* from the shelf, running a hand over the worn binding. That had been one of his favorites. He'd read it so many times he was sure if he gave it some thought, he could recite it word for word from memory.

"I love the smell of paper and leather, don't you?" She raised the book to her nose and inhaled. "Hmm, it reminds me of weekends at my grandfather's house. He owned lots of books, too. But not this many."

Pete wheeled himself closer, mesmerized. Something about her was so familiar, yet he hadn't even seen her face. "Who are you?"

She carefully returned the book to its place on the shelf. "Considering that little tantrum you just pulled with your parents, I suppose you could say I'm your worst nightmare."

As she turned to him, Pete had to remind himself to breathe. Worst nightmare? Hardly. She looked more like a wet-dream fantasy. Short dark hair hung in soft ringlets around a lovely heart-shaped face—

Lovely? Good God, where had he dredged that up from? He wasn't the kind of man to use a word like *lovely,* though he had to admit the description fit. She was sharp, too. He could clearly see the spark of intelligence in her eyes. They were round and dark and shone with a cockiness he used to see when he looked in the mirror. She also looked very familiar.

"Do I know you?"

"You know that taking your anger out on your parents isn't very constructive," she said. "You should channel those emotions into your recovery."

He frowned. "What are you, a shrink?"

"God, no," she said with a short burst of silvery laughter. "I'm going to teach you how to use that new knee. I'm Maggie Holm, your physical therapist."

Maggie followed her newest patient as he wheeled himself out the door, amazed by the speed with which he made his getaway. He sure could move fast when he had something to run from. It had been difficult not to exhibit the surprise she'd felt at the drastic physical changes since she'd last seen him in the hospital cafeteria line. At that time, they'd only said a brief and perfunctory hello. But throughout her lunch break she'd sneaked glances at him every so often, at the meticulously sculptured physique he must have worked years in the weight room to perfect. He was, in every sense of the word, a hunk.

And nice. He'd never carried himself with that air of authoritative arrogance so common to doctors. Pete was friendly and easygoing. There was hardly a time when he hadn't been smiling.

He wasn't smiling now. Today, if she'd seen him on the street, she might not have recognized him—sort of like he hadn't recognized her. Not that many men had given her a second glance back then. Not with the spare forty pounds she'd been hauling around. They'd both changed considerably.

His changes weren't necessarily for the better.

The Pete who sat before her today wore a wrinkled T-shirt and loose sweatpants, and his wavy dark hair was more than a little shaggy around the ears. Absent was the perpetually cheerful demeanor she remembered and the larger-than-life aura he'd once radiated like a beacon. Deep lines creased his forehead and brow, making him look years older than thirty-one.

She followed quietly behind him, gauging the amount of muscle mass he'd lost in the four months since the shooting. Though his physique was still above average on a normal scale, he'd lost more than a few inches in his upper body alone. That had to be a blow to his ego. She nearly cringed at the thought of what the inactivity had done to his legs, and at the grueling work ahead. Even worse—given his rotten attitude—she had to determine the proper method of motivation.

A cattle prod came to mind.

He glanced over his shoulder at her and smirked. "Are you still here?"

She regarded him with a pleasant smile. "I'm sorry, did you want me to leave? I thought you were giving me a tour of the house."

He stopped and turned. "Look, I appreciate that you have a job to do, but you're wasting your time here."

"I disagree," she said.

"You do?" His eyebrows quirked up and for a second she saw a glimpse of the old Pete, the one hiding behind the sarcasm. *Phew.* At least he was still in there somewhere. Now she just had to find a way to draw him out, to turn his anger around and use it constructively.

She chuckled to herself. She did sound like a shrink, didn't she?

"Yes, I do," she said. "I'm going to get your stubborn behind out of that chair."

His jaw tensed. "Suppose I don't want to walk?"

She shrugged. "That's never stopped me before."

He wheeled around and continued down the hall.

She followed him. "I've seen your file. Total knee replacement. You've lost bone, making your left leg slightly shorter than the right, and you've suffered some minor permanent nerve damage. I've seen worse. I've had sixty-year-old women with both knees replaced and you can hardly tell. Don't tell me you have less stamina than a sixty-year-old woman."

His back straightened just a little at the jab. "This is not about stamina. I'm never going to have full use of my leg."

"No, you won't."

He glanced back at her, a look of surprise on his face.

"What? Did you think I was going to lie and say you would

make a total recovery? I'm a good therapist, doc, but I'm not that good. Not to mention that your attitude sucks."

He hung a right into a large suite at the end of the hall. She sidled in behind him before he could slam the door in her face. She was sure that was exactly what he had been planning to do.

Gazing around the room, her eyes widened. Yow! What a spread. The sitting room alone was larger than her entire apartment. Hell, it was probably larger than the entire first floor of her parents' house. The room was extravagantly decorated in rich shades of green and mauve, ostentatious Oriental rugs covered the polished wood floors and heavy velvet drapes hung in arched windows that kissed the peak of the cathedral ceiling. It was a bit on the gaudy side—as in gag-me-with-a-fork gaudy—and she couldn't help thinking how out of place Pete looked there. She'd pictured him in something a little less…well, *ugly*.

She wandered toward the adjoining bedroom and peered in. It was even worse. The same ugly drapes were drawn, making the room dark and foreboding, like an oversized tomb. The cherry furniture looked antique, with the exception of the hospital bed that stuck out like a sore thumb. It sat low to the ground with a bar overhead to help him lift himself in and out.

Completely unnecessary, she thought. His legs were probably stiff and weak, but there was no good reason why he couldn't use them to hoist himself in and out of bed.

She glanced over and saw that Pete was watching her. "May I?" she asked, gesturing to the bedroom.

"Would it do me any good to try and stop you?"

"You could try," she said. "But I'm pretty fast."

He shrugged. "I don't know what you expect to find in there."

Neither did she. But it wouldn't hurt to look.

She stepped inside. As far as she could see, no personal effects had been set out to give the room character. In fact, it reminded her an awful lot of a hotel room. That alone spoke volumes about his frame of mind. Though he showed no interest in getting on with his life, he lived in an environment that looked awfully temporary.

She checked the bathroom next. Every conceivable amenity had been added to make it wheelchair-friendly. The sink and counter were wheelchair height and a shower seat sat in the stall. The whole suite would be just dandy for a paraplegic, or a man who'd had both legs amputated. Pete was neither.

By trying to make his life easier, his parents had given him no incentive to fight.

Unfortunately, that wasn't uncommon. Parents, no matter how good their intentions, just seemed to have a way of messing their kids up.

Like her parents' approach to dealing with their fat, out-of-control daughter. The disapproving looks when she reached for that second roll at dinner. Allowing her half the food they let her thin older sister pile on her plate, then wondering why she would sneak into the kitchen in the middle of the night and gorge herself. The lone bag of raw vegetables and bottle of water she'd find in her school lunch every day when the other kids had peanut butter and jelly with chips and granola bars.

The absolute worst, most humiliating form of torture her parents had dished out had been the summers spent at fat camp. She used to dread the end of the school year, knowing she would be shipped off to that horrible place. And then there was the even more ghastly experience of coming home at the end of summer and seeing the disappointment on her parents' faces when she hadn't magically become thin and beautiful like her older sister Molly.

"Another five hundred down the drain!" her mother would bluster in front of God and everyone. "Margaret Jane, I swear you're going to be the death of me."

She felt a familiar jab of resentment and knocked it back down. Now was not the time to mentally rehash her very dysfunctional childhood.

She walked out of the bedroom, and Pete was sitting by the window with a faraway, almost yearning look on his face. His parents were right about one thing—he wouldn't be happy until he was up and moving again. He just had to learn to accept his disabilities, to accept himself as imperfect. For a man like Peter, a man who had once personified perfect, that could be difficult.

She stepped up behind him, gazing out upon a picture-perfect garden. A cobblestone path wound its way through lush flower beds exploding with vibrant color; trees swayed lazily in the gentle summer breeze amid acres upon acres of rolling green grass.

"It's beautiful," she said.

"I guess."

"Do you get out there much?"

"The path is too narrow for the chair."

"I noticed a pool on the other side of the yard. Swimming would be good for your leg."

He looked up at her, his expression blank. "Seen enough?"

"Of what?"

He spread his arms out toward the room. "Of this—my life. If you're finished, you can go. I don't mean to be rude, but it's time for my nap."

"You don't mean to be rude? Isn't that *exactly* what you mean to be?" she asked, and he shrugged. "Knock yourself out, doc. I'm pretty tough."

He glared up at her, eyes like daggers. "Get out."

She folded her arms over her chest. "Okay, tough guy. Make me."

Two

The anger on Pete's face slipped for an instant. "Come again?"

"I said, make me. What are you going to do, pick me up and throw me out? You can't walk, remember?"

"That's very cute," he said. "Is that some sort of warped reverse psychology? Am I supposed to jump up and miraculously walk across the room now?"

She slammed her hands down on the armrests of his chair, caging him in, getting right in his face—and boy, did he smell good, just like she'd always imagined he would. A clean, masculine scent.

"Look, doc, for all I care, you can rot in that chair. I'm doing this for your parents, who I realize are not what you would call warm and fuzzy, but who seem to genuinely care about you. They think you'll make a full recovery, which, let's face it, we both know isn't gonna happen. You'll have a limp, possibly to the point of needing a cane to negotiate certain situations, or it may barely be recognizable. And of course you can look forward to more surgeries and physical therapy in the future, since that knee is only good for about ten years—fifteen if you're lucky.

"How you do all depends on how hard you're willing to work. Then again, maybe you won't work at all. You'll sit in that chair feeling sorry for yourself until every muscle has atrophied beyond repair and you never walk again. It's your choice."

His face remained stoic, but his Adam's apple bobbed as he swallowed.

She straightened to her full five feet four inches, but didn't back away. She could tell that her presence made him uncomfortable. At well over six feet tall, he probably wasn't used to people towering over him. In many respects, it had to make him feel overpowered, if only subconsciously. It was very likely part of the reason he insisted on pushing everyone away.

That wouldn't work with her. She excelled at making a pest of herself.

A nerve in his jaw jumped and for a second he looked a lot like his father. "Did anyone ever tell you that your methods suck?"

She couldn't help but crack a smile. "Honey, I haven't even started. When I'm finished with you, you're going to either love me or hate me."

"I think I hate you already," he muttered.

"Hate me all you want, doc. As long as you bust your butt to get better. You've got people rooting for you."

"What people?"

"At the hospital. The people who used to be your friends."

"You work there?" A speck of recognition lit his eyes.

"In the PT department."

"I thought I recognized you." He took her in from head to toe. "But, didn't you used to—"

"Be enormous?" she interjected.

Pete rolled his eyes. Why was it that all women had such a warped self image? She may have been a little on the thick side, he honestly couldn't remember. What he did remember was her eyes. They were so bright and full of life. That he'd forgotten her was an indication of how empty his own life had become. "I was going to ask if you used to have long hair."

"Yep, down to my butt," she said, fingering the short dark spirals at her nape. "We should get started. We have a lot of work ahead of us. Your parents gave me a tour of the exercise room and showed me the equipment they've rented. It should be adequate."

Boy, she was stubborn. Hadn't he already told her he didn't want her help? Hadn't he asked her to leave? "I don't think you heard what I said."

She stepped behind him and grabbed the handles of his chair, leaning close to his ear. "Oh, I heard you. I'm just ignoring you."

Her warm breath tickled his ear, making it difficult to concentrate—until she started pushing him toward the door. Beautiful or not, she was ticking him off.

He grabbed the wheels, grinding them to a jerky halt. "Look, Maggie…."

"No, *you* look." She circled the chair, propping herself on his armrests again, getting in his face for the second time that day. If she were a man, he probably would have decked her by now. And if she were a man, he wouldn't be having such a hard time *not* looking down her shirt, which was fairly low-cut and just happened to be at eye level. Her chest was full and lush and lightly freckled across her cleavage. It was just...*wow*.

He couldn't stop himself from enjoying the view.

"I'm going to get you out of that chair, whether you like it or not," she said.

He tried to keep his gaze locked on her face. "So I can limp around and make a fool of myself? I don't think so."

"You don't mean to suggest that anyone with a limp is a fool? The thousands of men who come home from war with debilitating injuries are fools? Children born with crippling birth defects are fools?"

"That's different," he mumbled. He could see exactly what she was trying to do, but she didn't understand—anything less than perfect wasn't good enough. Not for him. Not for his parents.

And certainly not for Lizzy, his *ex*-fiancée.

"What do you plan to do with the rest of your life, doc? What about all those years you spent in college and medical school? Would you really throw all of that away because you're afraid?"

He narrowed his eyes. "Let's get one thing straight. I'm not afraid. I just don't do things halfway."

"Halfway?"

He looked away. "You wouldn't understand."

She arched her neck, forcing him to look at her. She had

the darkest eyes he'd ever seen, and so deep he could get lost in them. "Try me."

"I worked in the ER. The pace is fast and reaction time is critical. If I were to rejoin my staff in anything less than perfect physical condition, I would be compromising the integrity of the entire team. I can't, with a clear conscience, limp around the ER just hoping that I won't slow everyone else down."

Her eyes narrowed slightly. "And your colleagues, they've expressed their concern to you?"

"Not exactly. They would never come right out and say that to me, but I know what they're thinking."

"Really?" She looked intrigued. "Forget medicine altogether. You should look into a job at one of those psychic hotline places." She leaned closer, until it was almost impossible *not* to look at her breasts. They were just so right there in his face. "Tell me, doc, what am I thinking right now?"

He cleared his throat. "Given your track record today, I'd have to guess it's either rude or sarcastic."

Smiling, she backed away and he heaved a silent sigh of relief. He may have been a cripple, but he was still a man— a man who hadn't had the pleasure of a woman's company in four months. Four very *long* months.

"Actually, I was thinking that you smell great. It's that clean, crisp cologne that makes me think of camping in October. You know, just before the leaves start to fall. When it's not quite cold enough for winter coats, but a jacket is too light, and the heat of the campfire keeps you toasty warm. The kind of night to cuddle up in a sleeping bag with someone special and…well, you get the picture. Do you remember nights like that, doc?"

Unfortunately he did. Vividly. And he couldn't help imagining himself snuggled up, sharing a sleeping bag with someone like her.

He tried to swallow, realizing suddenly that his mouth had gone bone-dry. She was messing with his head. And she was good at it.

"You know what else I was thinking? If you really don't care what people think of you, why would you bother putting on cologne in the first place? Hell, why bother shaving? I was also wondering, if you no longer care about your career, why you were reading a medical journal when I came in earlier? Then I was thinking, if you're so content sitting in that chair, why does it bug the hell out of you every time I get close and you have to look up at me?"

Because I'm not used to having breasts shoved in my face? He couldn't very well say that now, could he? "You seem to have all the answers. Why don't you tell me?"

"You're afraid. You're afraid to be anything less than perfect. I'll let you in on a little secret, doc. You weren't perfect."

"Is that so?"

"You only think you were."

Pete glared up at her with piercing blue eyes—eyes filled with a world of hurt and horrors she could only imagine. Which was why she was even more determined to see this through. He seemed so close to cracking, but she wasn't quite there yet. So many people would be disappointed if she failed. She'd been chosen for this job because she had a reputation for dealing well with difficult clients. The man just didn't realize how much everyone at the hospital cared about him. She cared, too, probably too much for her own good—and his.

But whatever he could dish out, she could take. God knows she'd been through much worse.

She sat casually on the sofa, as if she didn't have a care in the world. "So what do you say, doc?"

Pete wheeled himself to the window behind her so she could no longer see him, but she couldn't miss the exasperation in his voice.

"I never thought I was perfect," he said. "And while your insight on my life is truly fascinating, you couldn't be further off base."

"Okay. Prove it."

"If I do, will you go away?"

The hopeful ring to his voice made her laugh. "Yeah, prove to me without a doubt that I'm completely wrong about you, that you don't need me, and I'll go away."

There was a pause, then he said, "Maggie, turn around."

Something about the way he said her name sent chills across her skin. She shifted around to see him and found herself looking directly at...his crotch? Her eyes traveled up all six-feet-however-many inches of him as he walked—okay, limped—around the couch, until he was *standing* in front of her. He was *standing*. Then he leaned down and wedged his hands on the back of the loveseat on either side of her head, caging her in. Instinctively she pressed herself deeper into the cushions and her heart started to pound like crazy.

Oh. My. God.

He leaned in close, until they were nose to nose, flashed her a cocky smile and said, "How do *you* like it?"

If her jaw hadn't been fixed to her skull it would have been lying in her lap. "You sneaky son of a bitch. You can walk!"

"Are you convinced?"

She scrambled from under his arm and jumped to her feet. "How long have you been walking?"

He lowered himself onto the arm of the sofa, wincing slightly as he brought his foot to rest on the floor. "A while. I use the equipment at night, when I'm sure I'll have some privacy."

She circled him, examining his knee, wishing she could get a better look. Now didn't seem the time to ask him to drop his pants. "What's your range of motion?"

"It's stiff, and total extension is still tough. Impossible really."

"Your muscles are short from all the weight lifting you used to do. You're not working with enough resistance. We'll fix that."

His eyes widened. *"We?"*

"Yes, *we.* You've done a lot on your own, but with my help there's no telling what you could accomplish. I thought you'd been sitting around letting your muscles deteriorate. This will cut months off your therapy. We should start today. *Right now.*"

"I can't do that," he said, his voice rich with resignation. "Not today. Not ever."

"What do you mean you can't? You've come so far. I want to help you. Everyone will be so thrilled—"

"No!" He shot up so fast that he lost his balance and almost fell into her. She grabbed hold of his arm to steady him, but he pushed her hand away. "I don't need your help, and I don't want you telling anyone anything. I don't want anyone seeing me this way."

At that moment it became perfectly clear. He was embarrassed. He didn't want anyone, not even his closest friends and family, to see him struggling. Pride was getting in the way of his recovery, making him feel he had to do it alone, when now, more than ever, he needed help. He needed the support of the people who cared about him. Didn't he understand that he could only take this so far on his own?

Obviously, he didn't. She could tell him that it didn't matter that he wasn't perfect, that he was still the same man inside. That when he stood, even on a bad leg, he was still a powerful presence. She could even tell him that when he'd pinned her to the couch like that it had made her heart go berserk, and that his classically handsome features still left her a little breathless. That seeing him in the hospital had always lifted her spirits, and often she would make excuses to visit the ER just to get a glimpse of him.

She could tell him that she almost didn't take him on as a patient, for fear that she was too emotionally attached. But she knew she would never have the guts to say it. Not only would it be completely unprofessional, she would never humiliate herself that way. He was a million miles out of her league.

"I'd like you to leave now," he said, hobbling back over to his chair and lowering himself into it. "I can do this on my own. And though I can't force you, I'd appreciate it if you didn't tell anyone what you saw today."

"You need me, doc. Deep down, you know that."

He wheeled himself toward the door. "I'm sure you can find your way out."

She was losing ground fast. It was time to pull out the *really* heavy artillery. "Is this what your fiancée would have wanted?"

He turned to her, his eyes blank. "Goodbye, Maggie. Thanks for stopping by."

Just like that, she'd lost the battle.

For now, anyway.

Three

Pete woke to the squeak of his bedroom door opening, but he was too tired to pry his eyes open.

"Go away," he mumbled, pulling the blanket to his chin, silently cursing whoever it was for rousing him from one of the most erotic dreams he'd had in his life.

He'd dreamed Maggie had stolen into his room in the middle of the night. She'd stripped for him in the burnished moonlight in front of the open window, her slinky form hardly more than a shadow, leaving his imagination to roam. Then she'd climbed into his bed and the dream had become a blur of soft skin and slick heat and intense sexual sensation. He'd just been getting to the really good part when—

"Morning, doc. Time to get up."

He groaned, opening one eye to find the object of his dream hovering over him. "You again?"

"Get out of bed."

He closed his eye and sighed. *Why don't you slide in here with me?* The aftereffects of the dream weren't lost when she'd roused him—or, more to the point, *a*roused him.

She poked him through the covers. "Come on, wake up. We have work to do."

"Get lost," he said, pulling the blankets over his head. He'd been up half the night using the PT equipment and his body ached from the vigorous workout. He wondered if she was trained in massage therapy....

Before he could ask, she tugged the covers down to his shoulders. "I'm not leaving until you're up."

Up? I'm up, all right. He peered at her through half-open lids, in time to see her reach out and grasp the covers, knowing exactly what she was about to do.

"I sleep in the—"

The covers flew off him. "Rise and sh—"

"—nude."

The comforter fell and came to rest somewhere south of his thighs.

"Ooops!" She slapped a hand over her eyes and spun around so fast, for a second she was a blur of denim and white cotton. "Sorry about that."

"I tried to warn you." He sat up and reached for the covers, pulling them to his waist.

"I guess I just assumed you would be wearing pajamas."

"Yeah, well, I don't."

"I see that."

"Do you wake all your clients up this way?" he asked, yawning and raking his fingers through his hair. "In the wee hours of the—" he glanced at the digital clock beside his bed "—afternoon."

"Most of my clients are up before one o'clock."

"I told you yesterday that I like to work out at night." She was still turned away, and he stole the opportunity to check out her behind. She was wearing another pair of snug jeans that flaunted every curve, and the arousal that had begun to ease was threatening to rise up for a repeat performance. Time for a change of scenery. "You can turn around."

"I apologize if I've embarrassed you," she said, facing him.

"I have nothing to be to be embarrassed about." He wrinkled his brow and lifted the covers, looking down. "Or do I?"

Maggie bit the inside of her cheek, trying hard not to blush. Yes, she deserved his teasing. It had been presumptuous of her to barge in and rip the covers off him, and it was a mistake she would certainly not be making again. But to admit that the glimpse she'd gotten of his…well, it had been enough to assure her that he indeed had nothing whatsoever, at all— even the least little bit—to be embarrassed about. As a matter of fact, she was thinking that he ought to be pretty darned proud of himself.

And would she tell him that? Hell no. It was imperative they keep the line between caregiver and patient abundantly clear, now more than ever considering the proposition she was about to toss at him.

"Are you asking for my professional opinion?" she said. "Because sexual therapy really isn't my area of expertise. But if you're concerned that you're…*inadequate,* I could get you the name of a good therapist."

The corners of his mouth quirked up into an honest-to-goodness grin. It wasn't a big grin, but it was a start. She'd forgotten how gorgeous he looked when he smiled. Too gorgeous, in fact. He was also uncovered from the waist up and his chest was…well, he hadn't lost quite as much muscle as she'd suspected. He was still nowhere near as bulked up as he'd been before, but—she held back a sigh—he looked better this way, as far as she was concerned.

And, she realized, she was standing there staring at him. She backed toward the door. "Why don't I wait out here for you while you get dressed?"

"What's the matter?" He eased the covers down. "Afraid you'll see something you like?"

She shrugged, trying to look uninterested. "Sorry, doc. I sort of feel like if you've seen one, you've seen them all." Her back hit the door and she groped for the handle, hoping he didn't notice her sudden loss of coordination. "Take your time."

"Just give me a minute or two to get dressed and brush my teeth," she heard him say, and as the door snapped shut, she could swear she heard him laugh.

Ugh! What was wrong with her? It was understandable that she had been awestruck by the guy four months ago, but now he was a patient and that kind of behavior was inexcusable. Of course, she didn't usually see her patients naked. Not to mention that the majority of her male patients were wrinkly, shriveled-up old men.

She planted herself on the sofa. Okay, Mags, get a grip. It's not like you've never seen a naked man before—an *aroused* naked man. A really aroused and gorgeous naked man. Aroused and gorgeous and—

Sheesh! Get over it already. She'd fallen for a patient before and it had been a disaster. She was never making that mistake again.

By the time the door to the bedroom opened and Pete wheeled himself out several minutes later, she was back in professional mode, and intended to stay that way.

"Stop right there," she said. "I want to see you walk again."

His brow furrowed. "What for?"

"Humor me, okay?"

He glanced at the door.

"Don't worry," she said. "I locked it. The only way anyone is going to see is if they scale the side of the house and peek in the windows. It's just us."

Pete blew out a frustrated breath. She looked awfully determined, and a long, drawn-out debate didn't sound like a whole lot of fun right now. He had the sneaking suspicion that he would lose, anyway.

He'd humor her, just this once.

Pushing himself up on the arms of the chair, he rose to his feet, wincing at the familiar sting as he put weight on his bad leg. He'd taken only a few unsteady steps when she vaulted herself up off the couch.

"No, no, no! Not like that!"

"Jeez," he said, startled by her outburst. "What did I do?"

"You're favoring your good leg. You'll never get used to the prosthetic if you don't use it."

"I can't put that much weight on it. It hurts like a sonofagun."

She circled him, her brow crinkled. "Straighten it out."

He grabbed hold of a table for support. "I can't."

"When you work out, do you spend much time stretching it?"

"A little. Mainly I've been trying to build the muscle back up."

A pained look crossed her face, and he saw her take a very long, deep breath. "Don't take this the wrong way, but are you out of your friggin' mind?"

He mirrored her irritation. "What's wrong with trying to build up the muscle? The stronger my leg, the better I'll walk, right?"

"You doctors can be so dumb sometimes." She pointed to the couch. "Sit."

"Get up, sit down, get up, sit down—this is worse than Sunday mass," he grumbled, but he hobbled over and sat down anyway. She cringed with every step.

"Okay, give me your leg," she said, kneeling in front of him. When he hesitated, she sighed loudly. "I'll give it back."

He lifted his leg and she grasped his calf firmly. Then she pulled and he nearly went through the roof. "*Hey!* That hurts!"

She gave him a satisfied smile. "Do you know why it hurts, doc?"

"Gee, I don't know, it might have something to do with you *pulling on it!*"

She popped the bottom snap on his exercise pants, then paused, glancing up at him. "May I?"

"What, you didn't see enough in the bedroom?"

"Funny." She yanked the pant leg open to his thigh. He waited for her to gasp at the angry red scar tissue surrounding his knee, but she didn't even flinch.

"You must have been a lot of fun in the hospital," she said, fingering the muscle. "The nurses must have loved you."

He stifled a grin. "When I left the ICU, they threw a party. They said I was a lot more fun when I was in a coma."

She laid a hand on his thigh, just above the knee, and eased his calf up, watching his face. "You were that bad?"

"Yeah, I was pretty bad." He winced and she eased back. "I was still in the angry stage of my recovery."

"It's a wonder the nurses didn't murder you in your sleep."

He let a smile slip through. "You know what they say about doctors making lousy patients."

She pulled the leg of his pants together and fastened the snaps. "That's the second time you've smiled today."

The fact that she'd noticed, that she cared, made him smile again. It was an odd sensation. So many of those muscles in his face hadn't been exercised in a very long time. "You're counting?" he asked.

"I wouldn't normally, but I get the feeling you don't do it very often." She gave his leg a pat, then sat next to him on the couch. "But you should, it's nice."

Her comment made him feel better than it should have. It shouldn't have mattered at all that she liked his smile, but at that moment in time, it meant everything.

Moments pass, he thought ruefully. "So, Maggie, what's your diagnosis?"

She drew her knee up and used it as a chin rest. "You need to cool it on the weights, doc. Now is not the time to be trying to look like He-Man. Not only are you working the wrong muscles and completely defeating the purpose of the exercises, but the muscles you should be extending are actually getting shorter. You need to work on stretching the leg first, then add some resistance. We'll work out a routine together."

"I told you—"

She held out a hand. "Before you get all defensive and cranky, hear me out, okay? I know you don't want people to know what you've been up to, but I have an idea."

He scrubbed a hand over his face, realizing belatedly that he never should have gotten out of bed. He should have known she would be impossible to get rid of once she'd infiltrated his afternoon. "Okay, what's your idea?"

"Have you ever been to Gaylord?"

"I've passed through on my way to the Upper Peninsula a few times. Why?"

"Have you ever been to Turtle Lake?"

He didn't like the sound of this. "I don't think so."

"And you don't know anyone there, right?"

"Not to my knowledge. Is there a point to this?"

She smiled brightly. "Then it'll be perfect."

He really wasn't liking the sound of this. "Perfect for what?"

"For us. You don't want people you know to see you during your rehabilitation, so the obvious solution would be to go somewhere else, right? You don't know anyone at Turtle Lake, so that makes it the perfect place to go."

"What did you mean by *us?*"

"I mean pack your bags, doc. We're going to spend the rest of the summer together at Turtle Lake."

He was off the couch in a millisecond. *"No way."*

"Give me one good reason why it isn't a great idea," she said. "My grandparents have a small place up there. It'll be perfect. I've already arranged for the other PTs to cover my regular patients."

He limped right past his chair toward the bedroom. "You want me to stay with your grandparents? I don't think so."

"It's not like they'll be there. They live in Florida year-round, but they keep the cottage so my parents and my sister and I can use it. It's right on the lake and it's semi-secluded. It's perfect."

"Nothing about this sounds perfect to me." He tried to close the door on her but she pushed it open and followed him. "Will you stop following me!"

"Nope. I'm going to come to your house every morning and follow your stubborn rear end around until you agree to come with me. I'll follow you around for the rest of your life if I have to."

He spun around, towering over her with a menacing glare. "You really would, wouldn't you? You would make my life miserable just to get your way."

She didn't even flinch. "You bet I will. I'll be here every morning when you wake up. For two hours a day you'll be stuck with me. I'll be your shadow, pal." She poked him in the chest with her index finger. "You may be stubborn, doc, but I'm worse."

She was going to be harder to shake loose than he'd thought. "Even if I wanted to, my parents would never go for it. They want me close by so they can frown at me and give me disapproving looks."

"Already taken care of. I discussed it with your parents before I came up here. It took a little bit of persuading, but they finally listened to reason."

"*My father,* the king of I'm-right-and-you're-wrong, listened to reason? Why do I find that hard to swallow?"

"By the time I finished explaining it all to him I had him convinced it was his idea in the first place, and your mother seems to agree with just about anything he says, so she wasn't too hard to sway. So, whaddaya say, doc? A few months up north?"

He was running out of excuses—and energy. "What about

your boyfriend? What will he think about you picking up and spending the summer with a stranger?"

"Don't have one. And you, doc, have run out of excuses."

His knee was beginning to throb, so he sat on the edge of the bed. "Give me a minute. I'm sure I can come up with something else."

She sat down next to him, close enough that he could feel the warmth of her arm next to his, though she wasn't quite touching him. "Believe it or not, I know how difficult this is for you. And frightening, and confusing. I want to help you." She laid a hand on his forearm, her voice barely above a whisper. "Let me help you."

He looked down at the fingers curled around his arm, disconcerted by the contrast between his pale, almost translucent skin and her rich, sun-burnished complexion. He'd become a ghost. A shadow of a man.

Was that really what he wanted?

Maybe a few months in a completely different atmosphere would do him some good. If he was looking for a compelling reason to go, he didn't have to look any further than the woman next to him. What man in his right mind would pass up a few months alone with a woman like Maggie?

The kind of man who knew that she deserved better—that she would expect it. To her, he was just another damaged human being she could fix. One that she was probably being paid well to fix. She'd said it herself yesterday, she didn't really care if he rotted in the chair, it was just a job to her. A paycheck.

But this wasn't about her. It was about him, and damn it, as much as he would have liked to deny it, he wanted his life back. Besides, if he did go, and failed, he'd be no worse off than he'd been before. Right? With her help, he'd at least have a chance.

"If you say no, I'll have to reduce myself to kidnapping. You don't want me to commit a felony, do you?"

An honest-to-goodness chuckle rose in his chest and it felt...good. It had been a long time since anyone had made him feel this way. "You win. When do we leave?"

Four

"Aren't you driving a little fast?"

Maggie gripped the steering wheel with both hands. It was all she could do to stop herself from wrapping them around Pete's neck and strangling him. He'd done nothing but complain since they left. She was driving too fast, or the music was too loud, or he didn't like the station she was playing. It was too hot in the car, or it was too cold.

He was *never* happy.

At the rate they were going, this was going to be a really long summer. "I'm going the same speed as everyone else."

He glanced at the speedometer. "I'd like to get there in one piece if you don't mind—and alive."

Yep, a *really* long summer.

"I'll get you there alive," she said, and added silently, if I don't kill you first. Although it would be really tough to strangle a guy who smelled so darned good. Maybe duct tape over the mouth would be the more practical solution. She was sure she had a roll in the back somewhere....

"When was the last time you cleaned in here?" he asked, nudging two empty diet-soda bottles under the seat with his foot.

Her grip on the steering wheel tightened and her knuckles went white, but she kept her mouth firmly shut. She knew he was just saying these things to annoy her, as some sort of revenge for dragging him from the safety of his suite.

He was scared.

"So what is this place called that you're taking me to?" he asked.

"Turtle Lake. It's about ten miles outside of Gaylord."

"You went there a lot when you were a kid?"

Maggie felt a familiar, deep sting of resentment. She'd spent *her* summers on the fat farm while her parents and sister went to the cottage. Until she turned fourteen and flat-out refused to go to that horrible place again.

"Not as often as I would have liked to," she told Pete.

"You have brothers and sisters?"

"One sister. Molly." The perfect child. The thin, pretty daughter who could do no wrong. Straight A's in school, valedictorian of her class—a feat she repeated in college. Met the perfect man five minutes after graduation and married him in a fairy-tale wedding complete with horse-drawn carriages. When Molly got pregnant six months later, Maggie secretly hoped she would balloon up to two hundred pounds, get horrible stretch marks and have fat ankles. Of course she didn't gain an ounce over the acceptable twenty-five pounds, and she'd lost it all by the time Maggie's niece was a month old—

complete with pancake-flat stomach. No stretch marks either, thank you, cocoa butter. Molly had the perfect body, the perfect husband, the perfect child, the perfect house. The perfect *life*.

It was so unfair.

"How about you?" she asked Pete. "Any brothers or sisters?"

"Only child."

"Were you spoiled?"

He shrugged, and looked out the window. "I was away at boarding school most of the time."

As they approached the exit for Gaylord, she merged over into the right lane. "Now there's a concept I've never understood. Why bother having kids if you're just going to ship them off to live somewhere else?"

"Never made much sense to me either, but as you pointed out, my parents aren't exactly warm and fuzzy."

She detected a distinct note of bitterness there. "I suppose you went to an Ivy League college, too."

"University of Michigan. I'll be paying off student loans for the next ten years."

"You paid for your own college?"

He flashed her a look, one that said back off. "Long story."

Point taken.

She took the exit for 32 and headed into town, passing the IGA and Wal-Mart, remembering they would need supplies. Although she doubted Pete was in any condition, physically or mentally, for a trip to the grocery store. On the way up she'd suggested stopping at a greasy spoon for lunch, but had to settle for drive-through fast food when he refused to get out of the car. Not that she was surprised. His confidence had been shattered. It would take him a while to get that back.

They had all summer.

She would get him settled in the cottage first, then make a trip back into town.

"Before we get there we should probably hammer out the specifics of living together," she told Pete.

He just smirked and shook his head.

"What?"

"I've never lived with a woman, much less one I've known for only three days. This is going to take some getting used to."

"You didn't live with your fiancée?"

He looked out the window again. "She came from a very traditional family. She wouldn't move in with me until we were married."

And from what Maggie had gleaned from the rumor mill at the hospital, she'd hit the road not long after the shooting. Maybe the prospect of having a disabled spouse was more than she'd bargained for. God knows, Maggie had seen it before, though the majority of spouses and significant others stood by their partners. The strong ones did, anyway.

"Well," she told Pete. "I don't do anyone's laundry but my own, I'm a lousy cook, and don't expect me to clean up after you. I think it's only fair that we share the chores."

When he didn't respond, she glanced over at him. His brow was furrowed. She knew exactly what he was thinking. "Give me a little credit, doc. I'm not going to ask you to do anything you're not physically capable of. We'll take it one day at a time, okay?"

He nodded and absently rubbed his knee.

"Maybe someday you'll tell me about it," she said.

"About what?"

"The shooting."

Not likely, Pete thought. He'd never talked to anyone about that day. They'd tried to get him to go to a shrink a couple of times—his parents had even had a few come out to the house—but he didn't need to rehash what he'd been through. God knows he'd been over it a thousand times in his mind—what he could have done differently. If he'd only run away from the sound of the gunfire and not toward it, if he hadn't stayed to work that double shift because half the staff was out with the flu. If only.

What happened had happened, and talking about it wouldn't change anything. It wouldn't give him back his knee, or make his colleague Rachel any less dead.

It was over and he was putting it all behind him.

"Interesting architecture," he said, noting the Bavarian theme and chalet-style buildings as they passed through the main part of town.

Maggie nodded. "Butt out. Gotcha."

At least she could take a hint. Although he still wasn't quite sure what to make of her. He'd tried, without much success, to push all of her buttons on the drive up. He didn't even do it on purpose anymore. He was just so used to antagonizing people, to pushing them away, it was second nature. But it made sense, if he was to be stuck with this woman for the entire summer, that he should at least make an attempt to be civil.

They exited town and hit a long stretch of green, rolling

farmland. The road twisted and turned for several miles, then Maggie veered the SUV down a narrow dirt road. She hadn't been kidding about the remote location. They appeared to be in the middle of nowhere.

Beyond the dense treeline and thick underbrush he caught occasional glimpses of a house here and there and flashes of shimmering blue water beyond. The scent of clean lake air washed over him. He used to love the water. It should have been soothing, yet it only reminded him of waterskiing and windsurfing and all the other things he could no longer do.

She followed the road about a half mile around the lake, then pulled onto a long dirt driveway. Weeping willow branches brushed the top of the SUV and dappled sunlight dotted the windshield. The trees opened up to deep-blue water—miles of it—and an endless stretch of clean white sand. The cottage was small and quaint and meticulously kept. The entire setting was picturesque—like a scene from *On Golden Pond*.

So why did a hollow, relentless ache settle deep in his chest?

Maybe because he'd just realized what he'd agreed to— an entire summer of torture. A summer to contemplate all he would never do again. And he couldn't back out. Not now. He was stuck here.

Wonderful.

"Home sweet home." Maggie pulled up in front of the cottage and cut the engine.

Pete opened the door and eased himself down. She'd insisted on leaving his chair back at his parents' house, so negotiating the uneven ground to get to the door was going to be tricky. He was still having a hell of a time putting any real weight on his leg.

"Stay right there," Maggie said, "I have something for you."

She walked around back, opened the hatch and fished something out, then continued around to his side. When he saw what she was holding he shook his head.

"*No way.* I refuse to use a cane."

"It's temporary. You need something to get you through the first couple of weeks, until we get that leg stretched out."

"I told you before, I am not going to limp around on a cane."

Maggie shrugged. "Have it your way. When I'm in town I'll stop by the medical supply and get you a walker."

He narrowed his eyes at her. "That's a joke, right?"

She shrugged again. "It's this or a walker, take your pick."

Oh, she was evil.

He looked down at the cane she was grasping. To her credit, it wasn't the silver, geriatric variety he often saw his older patients using. It was crafted from deeply stained cherry, with a gold band and a flat, ornately carved handle that showed a fair amount of wear.

"It was my grandfather's," she said, gazing at it with affection. "He used it for a couple years, before he needed a wheelchair, so it has sentimental value."

She was even more evil and scheming than he'd imagined. If he said no now, it would be some slight against this grandparent who she obviously held dear to her heart.

"He was your height, so it should be just about the right size," she coaxed, waving it in front of him.

Pure evil.

"Two weeks," he told her. "Two weeks and this thing goes in the closet."

"Whatever you say, doc," she agreed, handing it to him.

Tentatively, he reached out and took it from her.

"Do you know how to use it?"

He gave her an exasperated look.

"Save the sarcasm. It actually takes a fair amount of coordination. Particularly since you'll be using your left hand. You have to keep your steps in sync with the cane. To your benefit you have exceptional upper-body strength. You try it out while I take the bags inside."

Maggie disappeared behind the SUV and Pete gripped the cane in his left hand. It was comfortable, but strange and unfamiliar at the same time. He looked over to be sure Maggie wasn't watching—the last thing he needed right now was an audience—then took a few tentative steps, stumbling on the rocky ground. Damned if she wasn't right, it was difficult to coordinate his movements. His left hand wanted to swing forward with his right leg, but that meant his left leg bore the brunt of his weight. That was bad.

He tried again, slower this time, resting his weight on the cane as he stepped with his right leg, then, centering his weight on his right leg, he stepped with his left. He managed two successful steps before he nearly fell flat on his face.

Rather than let himself get discouraged, he took a deep breath and tried again. The afternoon sun beat down hard on his back, and sweat beaded his brow, but he was determined to get this right. If he could cross-country ski, he could do this, damn it.

Maggie watched Pete through the car window as she unloaded the bags. She knew if she could only get the cane in his hand, get him to try it, he would learn to use it. He was too proud not to. She also knew he wouldn't want her standing and watching, telling him what to do. He would want to figure it out for himself—which was both good and bad. And though he'd had a rough start and a bit of stumbling, already his steps were more in sync. What the cane would do, even more than aid his walking, was build his confidence. He would be able to move faster and worry less about stumbling or falling.

She watched the muscle in his bare left arm flex and contract as he moved slowly forward. His brow was knitted deeply in concentration and sweat had begun to soak through his shirt. He stumbled again, this time nearly taking a nose dive into the dirt, and she cringed. She wanted to run to his aid, but knew he'd only brush off her help. He needed to do this on his own. Stubborn bastard.

And she admired the hell out of him for it.

He stopped for a moment, both hands braced on the cane, and she wondered if that was it, if he'd had enough. He took a couple of deep breaths, straightened up and started over again. Then she had no doubt that he wouldn't stop until he'd perfected his technique. She breathed a quiet sigh of relief, hefted the last of the bags from the back and carried them to the door.

The truth was, it made her ache to see this once larger than life man so beaten down—and by his own pride. She would use whatever means were necessary, no matter how unconventional, to rehabilitate Pete, and when she'd taken him as far physically as she could, she was determined to make him see that living with a disability wouldn't make him less of a man.

Failure wasn't even an option.

Pete stretched and opened his eyes, disoriented at first by his unfamiliar surroundings. The cottage.

Dark paneled walls came into focus, lined with row upon row of framed family portraits. Red-checked curtains hung in wood-paned windows and a rickety wooden storm door led out to a screened-in side porch that overlooked Turtle Lake. The air was musty with a vague hint of some kind of flowery potpourri. It was all so…*quaint*. A pleasant change from his parents' mausoleum of a house.

On the rare occasion his parents had taken him along for family holidays, they'd stayed in five-star resorts and hotels. He tried to imagine his mother in a place like this, with no one to wait on her hand and foot. With no silk sheets, fine china or gourmet cuisine.

It was enough to make him grin.

He pushed himself to a sitting position on the threadbare old couch—which was a lot more comfortable than it looked—and glanced at his watch. He'd wandered around outside for a good hour after Maggie had left to get groceries, investigating his surroundings, practicing his new walk, until his arm trembled from the physical exertion. He hadn't meant to doze off, only to relax for a few minutes. But he felt surprisingly well-rested for having slept only an hour and a half. He was a little sore, but he felt, well, *good*. As if he'd actually accomplished something today. Something important.

The storm door squeaked on its hinges as Maggie stepped inside from the back porch. When she saw him sitting there, she smiled a bright, happy-to-see-you smile that instantly lifted his spirits. The body-hugging, low-cut tank top and short-shorts didn't hurt either. Her figure was above average with modest clothing on. Like this, she was…*wow*. On a scale of one to ten, she ranked right up there in the low twenties. Her breasts were full and round, and he'd bet his medical license they would feel fantastic pressed against his chest—or other places.

And if he didn't alter the direction of his thoughts, her body was going to raise more than his spirits.

"Well, look who's up," she said. "Have a good nap?"

He yawned and stretched. "Yeah, I didn't mean to doze off."

She gestured to the small kitchen at back of the cottage. "I got a bunch of deli meat and cheese and some whole grain bread if you're hungry."

"Maybe later," he said, looking for his cane, finding it just where he'd left it, on the floor beside the couch.

"In that case, would you like to join me for a swim?"

She didn't tack on the "it would be good for your leg" line, even though he knew she was thinking it. And knowing she was thinking it dashed his enthusiasm. Maybe he just didn't like someone telling him what to do. Or maybe it was because lately everything seemed to revolve around his disability. For once he would like to do something for the sake of doing it, not because it would be good for him. But he was stuck here, so he might as well make the best of it. The sooner he got on with the rehabilitation, the sooner he got on with his life.

Besides, a swim sounded pretty good.

"Yeah, I'll come with you," he said, using the cane to hoist himself up off the couch. "I just need a minute to find my swim trunks."

"Great. I'll meet you outside."

She disappeared into her room, and he hobbled into the adjacent bedroom and closed the door. It was on the small side and had the same dark paneling as the rest of the cabin. The full-size bed was made up with flowered sheets and a colorful hand-stitched quilt, and in the middle of it sat his bags.

He unzipped the one with his clothes and fished around for his swim trunks. He was tempted to take a moment to unpack and organize—a practice that had been hammered into him in boarding school. Instead he changed and grabbed a beach towel from the closet Maggie had pointed out to him earlier, then slowly navigated his way out the door to meet her on the beach. He'd pretty much mastered regular walking, but the wood steps from the porch proved to be another new challenge, as did walking on the beach. When he put weight on it, his cane sank deep in the sand, throwing him off balance.

Pete was so focused on not tipping over, he didn't notice Maggie standing knee-deep in the water. And when he did look up and see her, he was so stunned, he nearly fell flat on his face. He wasn't sure what he'd expected when she suggested they go swimming, but it sure as hell wasn't this.

She was wearing a bikini. And to call it brief would be a gross understatement. It was practically nonexistent. She might as well have gone out naked considering how little the four small, neon-yellow triangles covered. On a scale of one to ten, she'd just been bumped up to a solid thirty-five. Her breasts were perfect, her stomach smooth and flat, her arms and legs toned to perfection. She packed one hell of a body into that frame, even though in his opinion she was bordering on too thin. And though he was her patient, he was still a man.

He glanced up and down the beach, wondering who else might be enjoying the view. The only people he saw were too far away to get a good look. With the exception of a few boats slicing across the water, and a couple of swimmers here and there, the lake was practically deserted. He was guessing the area activities wouldn't really pick up until after the fourth of July—which was a mere week away. For now, the solitude would be nice.

Maggie turned her back to him and bent over, dipping her hands in the water, her bikini bottoms creeping further up her perfectly rounded backside. He wasn't sure what she was trying to prove dressing that way, or if she was trying to prove anything. Maybe it was a tactic she used for motivating her difficult patients—a definition he most definitely fell under. It would explain her impressive success rate. He'd done his homework, calling the hospital and inquiring about her reputation, and was told that indeed she was the best money could buy. Not that he'd expected any less from his parents.

Oh, if his parents could see her now…

Maybe this was normal for her. Maybe she was a nudist, and for her this was modest.

Either way, at this rate, it was going to be a really *long* summer.

Five

"The water's a little chilly," Maggie called out.

Oh good, Pete thought, peeling his eyes from her rear end. That would save him the hassle of a cold shower.

Although now that he thought about it, he hadn't considered *how* he would get into the lake. He didn't want to use the cane in the water and without it his leg hurt like hell, thanks to the vigorous workout earlier that afternoon.

"Come on," she called, waving him toward her.

"I better not," he called back. "I don't want to ruin your grandfather's cane."

"Here, let me help." Maggie waded toward him, her breasts swaying with every exaggerated step. "You can lean on me."

Oh yeah, Maggie's near-naked body pressed up against him. Don't think so. He took a retreating step. "If it's that cold, I think I'll skip it."

"Oh, don't be a wuss. It's not *that* cold."

Considering the tightly peaked nipples clearly visible through her bikini top, he would beg to differ.

She stepped up beside him and took his arm, wrapping it around her shoulders. Her other arm went around his back and her hand came to rest on his waist. The sexual urges that had lain dormant inside him for so long roared to life with a vengeance.

He couldn't do this. He couldn't touch her this way if they planned to keep the relationship professional.

"I really think I'd rather not," Pete said, attempting to lift his arm from her shoulder, trying to put a little space between them. "I don't want to hurt you."

"You won't hurt me," she insisted, gripping his wrist and molding herself up against him. "I'm a lot stronger than I look."

Aw hell, he could feel himself getting aroused, and with only swim trunks on, it was going to be real obvious in about thirty seconds if he didn't either get back into the cottage, or waist-deep in the water. And since the water was right there in front of him, that seemed the way to go.

"We'll take it slow," she said, easing forward, her grip on his waist tightening as he leaned his weight into her.

His right foot hit the water and he sucked in a breath. He usually only trekked into water this cold wearing a wet suit. "You call that a *little* chilly? It's freezing!"

"If you take it slow, you'll adjust." She took another step, urging him forward, then another, until the water reached his calves. She smelled exotic, like pure sex, and her right breast was cozied up against his side, which made concentrating on his steps more than a little difficult. Kind of like impossible.

Which would explain why he stumbled, losing his balance, and though Maggie was strong, he outweighed her by at least half. Once they started to go down she was helpless to stop it. And because their arms were wrapped around each other, they plunged face first in the water.

Frantically untangling themselves from one another, they both sat up, gasping at the shock of the extreme cold. It was like being tossed headfirst into a tub of ice. On the bright side, any concern Pete had of a conspicuous erection was doused by the frigid water.

This was a hell of a lot more effective than a cold shower.

"Or, we could just dive right in," Maggie wheezed, shaking the water from her hair. Holy cow, that was cold.

Pete slicked his hair back from his face. "I guess you're not as strong as you thought, huh?"

"I am so sorry." She put her hand on his bad leg. "Are you hurt?"

"Nope. Just cold and wet."

"This is my fault," Maggie said. "I shouldn't have pushed you to do something you weren't ready for."

"It's okay. No harm done."

She still felt guilty. She didn't know what had happened exactly. She should have been able to hold Pete upright. But when he had started to lean forward, her equilibrium had been thrown completely out of whack and she'd lost her balance. He could have been hurt.

But boy, did he look good sitting there, chest glistening in the sunlight. Even if he did have the pallor of the undead. The guy could really benefit from a couple of hours in the sun. Despite that, when they'd stood so close a minute ago, arms around each other, she'd felt the patient/physician line growing fuzzy. It must have been residual feelings from her former crush, when Pete hadn't even known she was alive.

Considering the looks he kept sneaking in the direction of her breasts, he noticed her now. Now that it was too late. Now that an intimate relationship would be immoral. Besides, she was sure he was only staring at her breasts because they were convenient, and he probably hadn't seen any for a while, locked up in the house the way he'd been. So in other words, he'd have been happy looking at any old pair of boobs, not necessarily hers.

Which made her feel worse instead of better.

What on earth was wrong with her? Physical contact was an integral part of therapy and it had never bothered her before. Not that she was *bothered* per se, just a little more *aware* than usual.

"You know what's really going to be fun?" he asked, goose bumps forming on his arms. "Getting me out of here."

"Do you think you can get up?"

"Honestly, I don't know. But if I don't get up soon, I'm going to turn blue."

She was beginning to shiver herself. "I guess it was a little bit colder than I thought. It doesn't really warm up until mid-July."

"That would have been nice to know."

"I could get the cane."

He shook his head. "It's an heirloom. I don't want to ruin it. Why don't you try pulling me up to my feet?"

"Are you sure?"

"I don't exactly relish the idea of crawling up to the sand. In fact, I don't even know if I *can* crawl."

Maggie pushed herself to her feet, bracing herself against a wave of dizziness. What the devil was wrong with her? It wasn't like her to lose her balance this way. Maybe it was hormones or pheromones or something.

Pete grabbed her hand. "You okay?"

"Yeah," she gave her head a little shake. "Just stood up too fast. Must be the cold." The late-afternoon breeze kissed her icy skin and she shivered. When she was sure she had her bearings, she held out her hands. "Okay, I want you to take my hands—and get a good grip. On the count of three, push up with your good leg and I'll pull you to you feet. If you feel yourself falling, just grab a hold of me and I'll steady you."

He shook his head in obvious disgust. "Christ, I'm glad no one can see us."

She would tell him he had nothing to be ashamed about—that his surviving the shooting was nothing short of a miracle—but she knew that wasn't what he wanted to hear. She held out her hands and he grasped them. "On the count of three. You ready?"

He gripped her firmly and nodded.

"Okay. One…two…three!" She pulled hard on his arms and he pushed off with his good leg, propelling himself upward. When he was upright and starting to tip forward, Maggie countered the action by stepping into him, arms around his back so she could steady him. Which put her at eye level with his throat—man, was he tall, and he weighed a ton. Nowhere near the one hundred and seventy-five pounds they'd recorded on his chart. She was guessing he was closer to two hundred—and not an ounce of that was fat. With him pressed against her, she could feel nothing but lean muscle flexing and contracting under her palms as he struggled to steady himself. His arms had circled her. One hand curled around her shoulder while the other rested firmly on her hip. So much skin touching skin.

A sizzle of awareness zinged through her bloodstream. She used to fantasize about Pete holding her this way—about what it would feel like. Fantasy paled in comparison to the real thing.

A good reason to let go.

"Well, you're up," she said, trying to ease back, but Pete held her firmly against him. God, did he feel good. She wanted to run her hands up his back, down his arms. She wanted to touch him all over.

Back away, she warned herself. But when she tried, he held on tight. "Um, Pete?"

He rested his chin on the top of her head. "Yeah?"

"Since you're up now, maybe you should let go?"

The hand on her hip tightened and wandered an inch or two lower. "I probably should. But it's been a long time."

"Since what?"

"Since I've held a woman this way."

You're just convenient, she told herself. He doesn't really want you. That didn't stop her legs from going soft, her head from feeling dizzy.

"You have to try not to think of me that way," she said. "I'm not a woman, just a therapist. Non-sexual. There's no reason to think of me as anything else."

"There are two pretty good reasons, and they're pressing against my chest."

Oh. My. God. "You know we can't do this. You're my patient."

He sighed, slow and deep. "I know. It just feels nice. I guess I missed it more than I realized."

"That will pass," she assured him. She would know. It had been quite a while for her, too. But as time passed, she began to lose that craving for physical contact, that need to be close to someone. She instead sated her craving for intimacy with books and movies and casual friendships.

He finally loosened his grip and she slipped under his left arm, so he could keep the brunt of his weight off his bad leg. Very slowly they made their way to the beach. Though it was only a few feet, it took several minutes, and she could see that he was in a considerable amount of pain. This had been a really bad judgment call on her part. For about a hundred different reasons.

When they reached the sand, she grabbed his cane and handed it to him, then helped him up to the cottage. When they were inside, Pete seated on the couch, she breathed a quiet sigh of relief. Only then did she really look at him and see the stark frustration on his face.

"I know you probably won't believe this, but you're doing really well, doc." She sat beside him. "It's just going to take time. We pushed a little too hard today."

He leaned his head back and closed his eyes.

She had the distinct feeling she was losing him, that he was going to give up before they had even gotten started. "First thing tomorrow we'll start stretching that leg. You'll be amazed what a difference it'll make."

He nodded.

The sarcasm and the bad attitude she could handle. It meant he was still feisty, still prepared to fight. The silence scared her. If he turned in on himself, she might not have the skills to draw him back out.

They had taken a huge step backward today, and she couldn't help feeling that she'd failed him somehow.

"Sonofabitch." *Pete peeled the blood-coated latex gloves from his hands and tossed them on the floor. "Time of death, 11:36 p.m."*

The metallic stench of blood filled the room—from the body of a fifteen-year-old who'd come in moments ago, his body riddled with bullets.

"He was too far gone, Pete." Rachel Weathers, the doctor assisting him, shook her head sadly. "He was a gang member, this was bound to happen sooner or later."

While the rest of the team cleared the room, Pete grabbed the kid's chart off the rack by the door. His student ID was clipped on top: Simon Richards, ninth grade. Jesus. They seemed to get younger and younger every year.

"Did his buddy make it?" he asked Rachel.

"You mean the one he blew two holes into? They took him up to surgery a few minutes ago. One bullet nicked his left ventricle and another shattered his spine. If he lives he'll be a quadriplegic."

Pete pinched the bridge of his nose. At times like this he almost wished he'd become a pediatrician or a dermatologist, though he knew, if given a choice, he wouldn't trade this for anything. Here in the ER, he knew he was making a difference, he was saving lives. Well, usually he saved lives. On nights like tonight the multiple traumas, the senseless violence, made him wonder why they bothered.

Rachel took the chart from his hands. "When word gets out what happened, there will probably be retaliation, which means more bodies. Why don't you run down to the cafeteria and grab us a bite to eat," she said. "You look like you could use a break. I'll hold down the fort until you get back."

He nodded, trying to remember the last time he'd eaten and, because he couldn't recall, determined that it had probably been too long. "Fruit salad?" he asked.

"And an Evian. Take your time, okay?"

He peeled the shoe guards off his feet, tossing them in the hazardous waste barrel, and started down the hall toward the elevator.

"Hey," Rachel called after him. "I'm seeing that new intern up in OB. Why don't we double for drinks tomorrow night?"

"I promised Lizzy I'd teach her how to water ski," he called back.

"In February?"

"Her parents have a place in Florida. We're flying down for the day."

"Didn't you guys just go rock climbing?"

"That was last month," he said, walking backward toward the elevator.

Rachel laughed. "You're going to wear the poor girl out before you make it to the altar—or is that the idea?"

Pete shook his head and smiled, watching as she disappeared around the corner. She knew as well as everyone else that he couldn't wait to get married and settle down.

He raised his hand to press the elevator button when he heard a loud pop—

Pete's eyes flew open and he sat up in bed, the last remnants of the dream clinging like a malignancy in his mind, his breath coming sharp and fast. Fingers of light slipped past the curtains and birds chirped outside the bedroom window.

He was safe in the cottage. Nothing bad could happen to him here.

It had been weeks since he'd had the dream. At least this time he'd been able to stop it before it got to the bad part. Before he relived the shooting, when he saw Rachel's lifeless body sprawled across the hallway.

If only he hadn't taken a break, he might have gotten to her sooner. Or if he'd been there with her, it might have been him instead…

He shook the thought from his head. He wasn't even going to go there. He'd already run it through his mind a million times and the conclusion was always the same.

He'd let his best friend die.

Tossing back the covers, he sat up and swung his legs over the edge of the bed. Cool, fresh lake air rustled the curtains as he grabbed his cane and hoisted himself up. His arm was still a little sore and his knee ached from yesterday's escapade, but he was determined not to let it get him down. He threw on a T-shirt and a pair of shorts and straightened the covers on the bed.

He glanced across the hall into Maggie's room and found it empty. Clothes were strewn everywhere, the covers on her bed a disheveled mess, and two half-unpacked bags sat beside the bed, their contents spilling over onto the wood floor.

He brushed his teeth and cleaned up, then headed out to the kitchen. She wasn't there either, but he found evidence of her breakfast. An open, half-empty container of low-fat cottage cheese sat on the counter next to a bowl of fruit salad half-covered with plastic wrap. Beside that sat a dirty bowl and spoon that she obviously hadn't bothered to wash.

Either she'd been in an awfully big rush to leave—although he couldn't imagine what pressing business she could have at eight in the morning—or she was a slob. Judging from the condition of her room, and the junk littering the inside of her SUV, he was guessing it was the latter.

He looked out back but didn't see her anywhere. Where the hell had she gone? At least the SUV was still parked out front, meaning she hadn't taken off on him. Not that he thought she would. She seemed pretty determined to keep him motivated. She'd looked downright complacent after the lake fiasco yesterday. It was obvious she blamed herself for pushing him too hard.

He only blamed himself. And he'd be a liar if he tried to tell himself he hadn't been damned close to giving up. It seemed as if, lately, his life was one disappointment, one frustrating setback after another. But yesterday he'd made some real progress. Feeling the sun beating down on his shoulders, the wind in his hair, the length of a soft, warm female body pressed against him, had made him feel the tiniest hint of his old self, the Pete he thought had died on that cold hospital floor alongside Rachel.

As always when he remembered Rachel, a shaft of pain sliced through his heart. She'd barely finished her residency, and was by far one of the most promising medical students he'd had the pleasure of working with. Working with her had made the long, seemingly endless double shifts so much easier to tolerate. It had been fun.

But no matter how adamantly he'd denied any romantic feelings toward Rachel, his fiancée, Lizzy, had been jealous of their friendship. She had always been terribly insecure, always fishing for compliments, needing reassurances that she was the center of his universe.

Pete swore that after he was released from the hospital, Lizzy had been relieved that Rachel was no longer around. All she talked about for those first few weeks was everything they would do when his leg was better. When he was back to normal. The sight of his healing wounds had appalled her. She was much happier pretending it was all a bad dream that would soon end.

It hadn't taken her long to grow frustrated by his slow recovery. For the first time in their year-long relationship the focus was no longer centered on her. Every day he didn't make a miraculous recovery, her aggravation grew more keen. Her mounting resentment hung like a lead curtain between them until he finally recognized the truth—less than perfect would never be good enough for her. She would never be satisfied married to a man with a permanent disability.

When he'd asked her to leave and never come back, sparing her the guilt of being the one to end the relationship, behind the hurt and rejection, he saw relief in her eyes. And somewhere deep down, he'd been relieved, too.

That was all in the past, he reminded himself. There was no point in dwelling on something he couldn't or wouldn't want to change.

Figuring the food would spoil left out in the heat, he put the cottage cheese and fruit in the fridge, then propped his cane in the corner and washed the dirty dish and spoon. He was just finishing up when the porch door opened and Maggie came through. He turned to ask her where she'd been, but all the air backed up in his lungs, making it temporarily impossible to speak.

She was wearing a pair of running shorts that hugged her like a second skin and a matching sport bra that crushed her breasts together to form a deep cleft. Man, did she have the cleavage, and she didn't seem the least bit shy about showing it off. Both items of clothing were soaked with sweat and her hair hung in damp ringlets around her face. When she saw him, she smiled.

"Morning, doc. You just get up?"

"Yeah. Looks like you got an early start."

"Up at the crack of dawn. I do forty-five minutes with free weights and jog for an hour every morning."

He used to jog, too. That was one more thing he would never do again.

Maggie joined him in the kitchen, opening the fridge and taking out a bottle of water. She smelled of sweat and sun and fresh air—a tantalizing combination. She threw back her head and took a long swallow of water, exposing her long, slender neck. There was something about her that was just so…elegant, despite her tendency to be sarcastic and downright belligerent.

The truth was, that was what he found so attractive. Her spunk, her zest for life and her passion. And he *did* find her attractive. There was no denying that. A man would have to be blind not to find a woman like Maggie desirable.

She dragged a hand across her sweaty brow, pushing her hair back from her forehead. "Have you eaten?"

"Not yet."

"I'd have a hearty breakfast if I were you. I'm going to work your tail off today."

He leaned against the counter. "I can hardly wait."

"Give me fifteen minutes to shower and change." She set the bottle and cap on the counter and trotted off to the bathroom.

Pete capped the water and put it back in the fridge. He found eggs, cheese and a variety of vegetables, so he fixed himself an omelet. He was just starting to clean up when Maggie reappeared, hair damp, dressed in a snug, low-cut tank top and terrycloth short-shorts.

Did the woman own a *single* modest article of clothing?

"Let's get started," she said.

"Give me a minute to clean up this mess." He set his dirty dishes in the sink.

"Just leave them. You can do it later."

"Why wait until later when it'll take me about two minutes to do it now?" he said, running the hot water and squeezing a drop of dish detergent on the sponge—both of which he found deep in the cabinet under the sink.

Maggie let out a long, exasperated sigh. "They're not going to go anywhere, you know."

"All the more reason to do it now." He scrubbed egg off his plate. "Then it won't be hanging over my head all morning."

"You mean there are men who voluntarily clean?"

"I can only speak for myself."

She propped her hip against the cupboard beside him and folded her arms under her breasts. "Well, I think you're some weird freak of nature."

"Gee, thanks."

"My mom would have needed dynamite to get my dad out of his chair to wash dishes. They're very traditional. She was a stay-at-home mom, and he's the breadwinner. She cooks and cleans and does the shopping, he works nine to five then sits in his chair and watches TV. How about your parents?"

"Boarding school, remember?" He rinsed the dishes and set them on the draining board. "I wasn't around to see what my parents did."

"Did it bother you? Being away from home, I mean."

"I hated being home. At least at school I had friends. Being home meant being alone."

"That's really sad," Maggie said, looking genuinely distressed. "And it explains why you had such a lousy attitude living there again. So many bad memories."

He was about to snap back with a sarcastic comment when he realized she was right. He'd been miserable. She'd done him a huge favor dragging him out of there. And he'd practically molested her on the beach yesterday. Talk about disrespectful. He was sure that catering to his overactive sexual urges wasn't part of the therapy, yet she'd been nothing but kind and patient and respectful. And he owed her a huge apology.

"Maggie, about yesterday—"

"No sweat. These things happen."

"I just want you to know, I have a lot of respect for you as a medical professional."

"You should. I'm damned good at what I do."

And only a little modest. He dried his hands and hung the dish towel on the refrigerator door. "Okay, I'm ready."

"I hope so, doc. We have a lot of lost time to make up for.

When I'm finished with you, you're going to be begging for mercy."

After all he'd been through, whatever she could dish out, he could take. "We'll just see about that."

Six

"**C**hrist, that hurts. Aren't we finished yet?"

"You know what they say, doc. No pain, no gain." Maggie knelt on a pillow in front of Pete, grasping his calf, extending his leg and stretching the muscle. Sweat rolled down the side of his face and he clutched the couch cushion with both hands. She bent his knee, giving him a few seconds to relax, then eased it straight, going as far as the short muscles would allow—then farther.

He gasped in a sharp breath. "Do you get off on torturing people?"

She eased back. "Oh, stop being a baby. For someone so macho, you sure have a low threshold for pain."

He scowled down at her. "I am *not* being a baby. You're stretching it too far."

They'd been at it for nearly two hours. First she did a full evaluation to gauge his condition and see exactly what he was capable of. The past hour they'd spent doing various stretching exercises to lengthen the muscles. Honestly, he was holding up pretty well considering how hard she was working him. The problem here was pride, and it wasn't uncommon. Even though he'd agreed to the therapy, he was still having a lot of trouble accepting her help. He didn't like anyone, even her, seeing him this way. Seeing him struggle.

It made him cranky.

"Has anyone ever told you that you have a lousy bedside manner?" Pete asked.

"Okay, is this better? Oh, you poor baby," she cooed and patted his leg. "Does that hurt?"

He fixed her with a look that could burn through concrete.

"Yeah, that's what I thought. Now stop whining and give me one more stretch. One more and I promise we'll stop."

"That's what you said five minutes ago."

"Yeah, well, this time I'm not lying." She grasped his calf firmly. "Come on, doc, one more."

"Like I have a choice," he grumbled, gripping the edge of the couch. Teeth gritted, he braced himself as she eased his leg up. She watched his eyes, noting the exact instant it started to hurt, holding his gaze. A bead of sweat rolled down the side of his face and dropped to his T-shirt. "Breathe through it, doc. Stay focused. Stay with me."

When she finally eased it back down, he collapsed against the cushions, breathing hard. "That's it, I'm done. My leg is toast."

"You did good." She rubbed her thumbs along his calf, massaging the muscle. She didn't want him cramping up. Now, *that* would hurt. "Now we get to do something fun."

"How about a nap? That sounds like fun."

"How about berry picking? There's a patch of wild rasp-berries about a mile up the road."

"Berry picking?"

"It'll be fun." She propped Pete's foot on her folded leg to lift it so she could reach the underside of his thigh. His skin was clammy from the intense workout, his leg hair crisp under her thumbs as she kneaded them into the muscle. The skin they had grafted onto his knee had healed well, but there would always be scars. She wondered how he felt about that—not that she didn't already have a good idea.

"You can stop now," Pete said from above her.

"We have to cool the muscle down," she said. "You don't want to cramp up."

"Maggie."

Something in the way he said her name gave her shivers. She looked up at him, at the intense, steel-blue eyes staring down at her, and her stomach did a flip-flop. He looked as though he might eat her alive.

"You really *need* to stop." Pete's eyes darkened a shade and Maggie's blood began to simmer.

"Massage is an important part of the therapy," she said, not removing her hands from his leg.

If he was uncomfortable with any part of the treatment, she should stop immediately. The problem was, he didn't look un-comfortable. He looked as if he was about two seconds from tearing her clothes off. Which was beyond inappropriate and completely unprofessional—so why was her heart beating a million miles an hour? Why did her head feel soft and fuzzy, her breasts tingly?

"I'm telling you this for your own good. It's been over four months since I've been with a woman, and I'm about fifteen seconds from doing something I shouldn't."

This was his fault really, forcing her into these casual circumstances. If they had been in a professional setting, in the therapy center at the hospital, she wouldn't be having all these inappropriate urges to touch him.

She wondered what he would do if she slid her hands farther up his thigh. Sitting nearly eye-level with his crotch, she could clearly see the effect this was having on him. She should have been embarrassed by her behavior, but all she felt was excited.

And naughty.

"Five seconds," Pete warned, sitting up, as if preparing to pounce. She could feel the muscles in his thigh tense under her fingers. She could see the fire in his eyes.

"Four…"

She really needed to pull her hands away, but felt frozen in place.

"Three…"

He was leaning forward, as if he were getting ready to kiss her.

"Two…"

Her lips tingled in anticipation, her head tipped to the right. *"One."*

What was she *doing?*

She yanked her hands away from his leg and sat back on her heels. "Sorry. That was unprofessional of me. If you were…*uncomfortable,* I should have stopped right away. It won't happen again."

Uncomfortable. That was a mild way to describe what he was feeling right now. If she hadn't pulled away that exact second, he'd have her on the floor right now, bad knee or not, professionalism be damned. She would never know just how close he'd been to tearing that skimpy top off her with his teeth.

"This is your fault," she said, but her voice sounded whispery and soft and he could see the flutter of her heartbeat at the base of her throat. She was just as excited by this as he was.

Interesting.

He sat back and folded his arms across his chest, not even trying to hide the fact that he was turned on, amused to see her eyes stray to his crotch, widen slightly, then dart away. "And how is it *my* fault?"

"This wouldn't happen back at the rehab center. The atmosphere here is too…casual."

He shrugged. "Hey, it was your idea to come here."

"Only because you wouldn't come to the hospital, or use the room in your parents' house. You didn't give me a choice."

It took an awful lot to ruffle her, but once she got her panties in a bunch, Maggie was a lot of fun to tease. "So you got fresh with a patient, it's not the end of the world."

She bristled at the accusation. "I did *not* get fresh with you. Massage is a part of the therapy. It's not my fault you have sensitive thighs."

"That's not the only thing I've got that's sensitive right now," he said, his gaze straying downward.

Maggie let out a snort. "What is this, *junior high?*"

"You have the hots for me. Admit it."

"In your dreams, pal." She stood up, grabbed the pillow she'd been kneeling on, and threw it at him. "You are *so* not my type."

He caught the pillow and laughed. As the sound filled his ears, he realized it was the first time since the shooting that he'd really laughed.

And damn, did it feel good.

But not nearly as good as Maggie's lush lips would feel against his own. Not nearly as good as her body had felt pressed against him as they'd stood in the icy water yesterday.

He wanted to feel that again.

He really shouldn't. He'd promised himself he would keep their relationship professional, but that was before he knew she was attracted to him. Before he realized how attracted he was to her. There was something about her, something that appealed to him, and it wasn't just her body. He *liked* her. And he had to know what it would feel like. What *she* would feel like.

No, he shouldn't, but he was going to anyway.

"Help me up?" he asked, holding his hand out. She grasped it and helped pull him to his feet. As soon as he was upright and steady, he cupped one hand behind her head, slipped his fingers through her dark, silky hair, lowered his head, and kissed her.

For a second she seemed too stunned to move. He waited for her to push him away, or possibly slap him. Instead, she sighed against his mouth. Her head tilted and her lips softened and she leaned into the kiss. Her lips were as soft and sweet as he'd imagined.

Just to see her reaction, he nipped her lip with his teeth. She whimpered and pressed herself against him.

He knew he should end it right there, but now that he'd come this far, he had to taste her. He touched his tongue to her lower lip.

She planted her hands on his chest, and he knew he'd gone too far. He waited for that inevitable shove, for her to push him away. Instead she curled her fingers into the fabric of his shirt. Her lips parted, inviting him in, and he would never turn down an invitation like that. Not from her.

Though he would have guessed her to be the take-charge type, she was almost shy as his tongue slid over hers. She tasted sweet and tangy and his insides instantly caught fire. He lost himself in the heat of her mouth, the softness of her body pressed against him. It was just so…sweet. So not like the aggressive, outspoken Maggie he was used to.

But to hold this sort of power over her, to alter the dynamics of their relationship, felt wrong somehow. Frankly, it scared the hell out of him. But man, he wanted her. He had to do something to break the mood, before this got out of hand.

He shifted her head so he could kiss his way along the line of her jaw up to her ear. She shivered in his arms.

"I told you," he whispered.

Her eyes were closed and she had a dreamy look on her face. "Told me what?"

"That you have the hots for me."

Her eyes slowly opened and she looked up at him, confused for a second, then her eyes narrowed and she shoved him back. "You kissed me just to prove you're *right?*"

Oh, if she only knew. Instead of gathering her back up in his arms and showing her what he was really feeling, he flashed her a slow, cocky grin.

"Oh, you are *low.*" She whirled around and stomped off, mumbling to herself, and Pete felt like slime. Despite his bad leg, it would seem he hadn't lost his ability to seduce a woman.

And if her reaction was any indication, he'd done a pretty fair job of hurting her, too.

"This is dumb."

Maggie looked back at Pete, filled with smug satisfaction. They'd been out there thirty minutes and he'd been complaining for twenty-nine. She watched him try to hold his cane and the metal pail while plucking wild raspberries off the bushes. He'd dropped the bucket four times, spilling his berries all over the ground, before he'd figured to hang the bucket on the wrist of the hand clutching the cane so he could pick with the other. She might have helped him if she didn't still feel like punching him in the nose.

That's what he got for messing with her.

She still couldn't believe she'd let him kiss her. That she'd been so susceptible to his charms. And as humiliated as she'd felt afterward, she recognized his behavior as a natural step in his recovery. He was reestablishing his sexuality, asserting himself as a man. She just happened to be the only female around to take up the slack.

That didn't mean she couldn't get a little good old-fashioned revenge.

"Dumb or not, we aren't leaving until your bucket is at least half full," she said. "Unless you want to walk back."

"There aren't that many berries here to pick."

"It's still early in the season. You have to look under the leaves. They like to hide."

Which would necessitate him bending and crouching, which was nearly impossible for him to do at this point. At the rate he was going, they might be out there all night.

"I'm getting eaten alive by mosquitoes," he complained. "If I get West Nile it's going to be all your fault."

"We put bug spray on."

"I must need more. Why don't you give me the keys to the truck and I'll go get it."

She gave him a how-stupid-do-you-think-I-am? look and he mumbled something about her being evil.

"This is your revenge for that kiss, isn't it?"

She just smiled at him.

"If I kissed you again, I'll bet I could talk you into driving me back."

She didn't doubt that he could. When he'd kissed her earlier, her brain had completely shorted out. He could have asked her to parade around naked on the beach and she probably would have done it.

"Keep those lips to yourself, buddy. There will be no more hanky-panky."

"You can't tell me you didn't enjoy it."

She plucked a few berries and dropped them in her pail. "That's completely beside the point. I'm a therapist and you're my patient. There are certain rules I have to follow. You're the last person on the planet I should be kissing."

"So you admit that you enjoyed it."

Did he really need an ego-stroking? Did he not have the slightest clue how gorgeous he was? How crazy he made her? "Yeah, doc, it was freaking wonderful—better than chocolate-covered cherries. But suppose an attractive woman came into the ER for treatment. Would you kiss her?"

"Of course not!"

"Then I rest my case." She set her pail on the ground behind her and crouched down to reach a cluster of low-hanging branches covered with juicy berries. She interpreted his following silence as a concession.

"I'm ready to go," he said a minute later.

"You wish." She dropped a handful of berries in her pail, and they landed in the bottom with a gentle thunk. "What the—"

Her pail was empty! Pete stood next to her, a look of complete innocence on his face, his own pail nearly filled to the top.

"You stole my berries! You cheater."

Pete shrugged. "You only said my pail had to be half full. You never said anything about me picking them myself."

She shook her head. "You'll stoop to any level, won't you?"

"There's something you should know about me, Maggie."

"Oh yeah, what's that?"

"When I set my mind on something I usually get it." He flashed her the sexy smile that made her heart beat faster, and pinned her with his steel-blue eyes. "And I always play dirty."

Pete raised his hand to press the elevator button when he heard a loud pop from the direction of the ER, as if someone had set off a firecracker.

"What the—" He spun toward the noise. Who would be dumb enough to blow off fireworks in a hospital? Light one a little too close to an oxygen tank and they would all be blown to kingdom come. Three more quick pops split the silence, followed by the shatter of breaking glass and a bloodcurdling

scream. Then all hell broke loose. People were rushing down the hall toward him, away from the ER. It took his mind several seconds to register that a few people were sprayed with blood, though no one appeared to be injured.

Instinct kicked in and his legs were moving on their own. He fought his way back toward triage as another round of popping reverberated through the halls. When he rounded the corner, he saw Rachel lying face-down in the hallway, a bright-red stain seeping across the back of her shirt.

"No!"

Pete woke with a start, sitting up on the couch. He was soaked with sweat and nausea churned his stomach.

It was the dream. It always made him feel nauseous.

He tried to swallow but his mouth was dry.

"You okay, doc?"

He turned his head, saw Maggie standing in the kitchen looking concerned. He caught the scent of seared beef drifting in from the back porch. He must have dozed off while she was making dinner.

"Yeah," he said, his voice raspy. "Bad dream. Could I have a glass of water?"

"Of course." She grabbed a bottle of water from the fridge and brought it over to him, sitting on the arm of the couch beside him.

He twisted the cap off and took a swallow, felt the nausea begin to ease, the swimmy feeling in his head clearing.

Maggie reached up, touched his forehead. "You're all sweaty. Are you sure you're okay?"

"Fine," he lied. "I'm fine. I probably just got too much sun this afternoon."

Though she didn't look altogether convinced, she didn't press the issue. "I was just about to wake you. Your steak is ready. I hope you're hungry."

"Starving," he said, even though the thought of eating anything right now was enough to gag him.

He grabbed his cane and pushed himself up from the couch, his legs—even his good one—feeling wobbly from all the exercise, and joined Maggie at the kitchen table. She'd fixed him an ear of corn that was slightly scorched on one end, a side salad, and an enormous, juicy steak. Looking at it, he felt the slightest twinge of hunger. "I thought you said you can't cook."

"Ask me to follow a recipe and I always forget some essential ingredient and ruin the entire thing. Tossing a steak on the grill, I can do."

"Where is yours?" he asked, gesturing to her lone salad.

"I don't eat beef."

"You're going to eat something other than lettuce, aren't you?"

"I'm not very hungry."

"You had cottage cheese and fruit for breakfast, a diet shake for lunch. When do you eat *real* food?"

"For me, this *is* real food. I'm still on a diet."

He looked her up and down. "What for?"

She folded her arms under her breasts and glared down at him. "If you think that's going to get you back on my good side, it won't work. I have no illusions about the way I look."

"I'm serious, Maggie. You look fine the way you are. Why would you want to lose more?"

"Only a former fat person can understand. I have a goal weight and I won't be happy until I reach it."

"Even if that means being *too* thin?"

She slid into the seat across from him. "There's no such thing as too thin."

Boy, was she wrong about that. "Apparently you've never seen any pictures of me when I was a kid."

"You were skinny?"

"In tenth grade I was six feet tall and weighed about a hundred and thirty pounds fully dressed."

She raised a skeptical brow. "*You* were that skinny?"

"I was a bean pole."

She stabbed a forkful of salad and shoveled it in her mouth. "So, what happened?"

"I got tired of the other kids teasing me, and the pretty girls ignoring me, so I started drinking protein shakes and going to the weight room every morning for half an hour before class. After about a month, when I really started to see results, I upped it to an hour.

"I joined the lacrosse team, started playing soccer. Girls started to notice me. By my senior year I was in the weight room every day by 4:00 a.m and again after classes for another hour or two. When I started college, I was six-three and weighed two-twenty."

"Which explains why all that muscle you lost since the shooting didn't turn to flab. You're naturally thin." She said it like he was some freak of nature.

"We're not so different, you know. You have to work to keep weight off, and I have to work to keep it on."

She speared her lettuce, staring at it with distaste. "Frankly, I'd rather have your problem."

"Maggie, you look great just the way you are, and I'm not

saying that just to get on your good side. I think it's pretty obvious I find you attractive."

Instead of being flattered by the compliment—which, *silly him,* he would have expected—she bristled with indignation. "And I must have seen you a hundred times in the hospital when I was fat, and you didn't look twice at me."

"I was engaged. I didn't look twice at anyone."

How did the guy always manage to say exactly the right thing? And if he loved his fiancée that much, he must have been devastated when she had ended the relationship. He had to be hurting, and she probably wasn't helping. She had to remind herself, as cocky and frustratingly charming as the guy could be, he'd been through hell, and there was a fine line even she couldn't cross.

She couldn't let it drop either.

"You still can't deny that looks are important to you," she said. "I saw your fiancée. She was gorgeous. You guys were the perfect couple."

Something flashed in his eyes. Not hurt exactly. Something darker. And she had the sinking feeling she'd pushed too far, that her toes had edged over the line.

"You can't believe everything you see, Maggie. Things are not always what they seem."

Seven

"**O**kay, push against my hand again. This time try to hold it."

Pete sat on the deck floor at the top of the stairs, his foot braced against Maggie, who knelt on the sand four steps down. Gripping the wood plank, he pushed with his leg, wincing as pain shot up to his knee. They'd been stretching the leg extensively every morning, and again in the evening, for ten days now, gradually adding resistance. It still hurt like hell though.

Between the stretching and resistance, the long walks on the beach she was taking him on every day and the swimming in the evenings, he had to admit he was walking better. So much so that he was getting a little antsy for the real therapy to begin.

Though he couldn't deny he enjoyed the time they spent together. He'd never been the long, casual stroll type—if it didn't make him sweat, what was the point?—but with Maggie it was different. She was easy to talk to and she had a good sense of humor. He *liked* talking to her. Sometimes they didn't even talk, they were just together. He liked just *being* with her.

He thought of all the things he and Lizzy had done together—the skiing and parasailing and cycling and a dozen other activities—but he couldn't recall a single time when they'd just sat together on a warm evening drinking iced tea and talked. He couldn't recall her laughing much, or making him laugh. Their relationship had been one of mutual respect and common interests. And whenever they did talk, it was usually about her law practice, or fashion or her latest hairstyle.

They'd never talked about things that mattered. About feelings. Now that he considered it, she was a lot like his parents in that way.

The thought gave him a cold chill.

Maggie, on the other hand, seemed to hold nothing back.

"Make sure you extend the leg as much as you can while you push," she said, and he tried to comply. Sweat poured from his forehead and dripped into his eyes. It was the second day in a row that the temperature had hit ninety before noon and the humidity was so thick the air sat like wet cotton in his lungs. He didn't dare complain though, or she would only point out that he wouldn't be melting in the heat if they were at the hospital PT center. That if he weren't so stubborn that's exactly where they would be.

And she would be right.

If the heat wasn't distracting enough, Maggie was wearing another low-cut, form-fitting tank and from his higher vantage point he could see right down the front it. He was trying hard not to stare at her openly, but come on, even he had his limits. Her skin was golden from the sun and lightly freckled. Her breasts were so full and round and soft-looking…

"You're not pushing." she said.

He tore his eyes away from her cleavage. "Sorry."

She abruptly let go of his leg. "If you're not even going to try!"

"I am trying," he said. "I just got distracted. It's your fault."

"How is it my fault?"

"Are you kidding? Look at you."

She looked down at herself. "Yeah? Here I am. What about it?"

"Your clothes," he said.

"Yes, I'm wearing clothes."

Man, was she a sass. "*Barely.* Your shorts couldn't be any shorter, and look at that shirt. If it were cut any lower you'd be falling out of it."

"What do you want me to wear? Jeans and a turtleneck?"

"What do you wear at the hospital?"

"Scrubs."

"So why don't you wear that?"

"What are you, a prude? You haven't noticed that it's about a million degrees out?"

"I just don't think it's very professional," he said, already seeing this was a losing battle. Once she got on the defensive, it was all over.

"*Professional?* You're one to talk, Mr. It's-too-hot-for-a-shirt. Did it not occur to you that seeing you half-naked might be a distraction to me?"

If it was, she sure didn't let it show. He was so used to women staring at him, her total lack of interest lately had been disconcerting. If what she said was true, and he *was* a distraction, she did a fair job of hiding it.

But hearing it straight from those luscious lips was a much-needed confidence boost.

"That's different," he said, knowing he was really going to get her hackles up now. In fact, he was kind of hoping he would. Though he felt like a degenerate for it, getting her panties in a twist was a major turn-on. "I'm a guy. Guys are supposed to go shirtless in hot weather."

She closed her eyes and took a long deep breath, as if gathering all her patience. "Look, doc, I worked hard for this body and I'll be damned if I'm going to cover it because you're a male chauvinist pig."

Pete suppressed a smile. "So you think we should be equal, that what's considered socially acceptable for me, should be the same for you?"

"Exactly," she said.

He shrugged. "Okay. Take it off."

A little wrinkle formed in her brow. "Take what off?"

"Your shirt. I don't want to be accused of being sexist. If you want to make this fair, we'll both do my therapy topless. Problem solved."

She looked as if she couldn't tell whether he was serious or poking fun at her. "You know that isn't what I meant."

"Hell, if you're that proud of your body, show it off. Here, I'll help." He grabbed his cane and boosted himself up.

Maggie rose to her feet, swaying a bit before she righted herself. "Sit back down, we're not finished."

He lowered himself down one step, toward her. "Not until the shirt comes off."

She watched him, eyes wary, as if she thought he might actually be serious. But she held her ground. "Like you really think I'm going to do your therapy topless."

He nodded thoughtfully, taking another step. This time she took a step back. "You're right, that probably would be a bad idea. Someone might see. There is still the issue of you distracting me though. Unless…"

Her eyes narrowed. "Unless what?"

"I think I know what we can do to fix the problem."

She propped her hands on her shapely hips. "I'm afraid to ask what that would entail."

"It's simple. You show me your breasts, then I'll know what they look like, then they won't distract me anymore."

She glared up at him. "You're enjoying yourself, aren't you?"

He stepped down onto the sand, right in front of her. "Although you know, once I see them, I'm going to want to touch them."

She was trying hard to keep her composure, but he could tell he was ruffling her feathers. Her pulse fluttered at the base of her neck and color climbed high up her cheeks.

The truth was, all this talk of her breasts was getting him hot. He'd been working hard to think of her in professional terms only. But after that kiss, after she'd practically melted in his arms, he was having a hell of a time. Maybe he should just say what the heck…

"Oh no you don't," Maggie said, her heart hammering about a million beats per second. He had that look again, the one he'd had when he kissed her.

She took an involuntary step back.

"Oh no I don't what?" he asked taking another step toward

her, until they were nearly touching, and she had to look *way* up to see his face. Why did he have to be so darned big? And why did he have to smell so delicious? Soap and sweat and man. It was doing funky things to her head.

"You look like you're going to kiss me. And if you try it, I'll have to do something drastic."

"Like what? Kiss me back?"

"Yeah, you wish."

"Yeah, I do," he said, and the hungry look in his eyes…suffice it to say, her knees instantly went weak. But she refused to back down, to let him get the best of her. Though somewhere, deep down, she wanted him to kiss her—she ached for it even. She could be happy kissing Pete every day for the rest of her life.

Oh yeah, like that's gonna happen, the rational part of her brain taunted. The man is so far out of your league. Why would he settle for a woman like you? You're just convenient.

"This isn't professional," she tried, knowing how lame it sounded. It didn't help that her voice was shaky.

"I won't tell if you don't." He reached up and touched her hair, wrapping one curly lock around his index finger. It made her think of the last time he'd kissed her, the way he'd slipped his fingers through her hair and cupped her head, taking control. How much she'd enjoyed being allowed to relinquish control for a while. Sometimes she got so tired of this driving need to keep the upper hand in all situations.

And he knew as well as she did, if she really didn't want him to kiss her, all she had to do was tell him. If she insisted, he would back off. Unfortunately the message was getting scrambled somewhere between her brain and her mouth.

Pete lowered his head and her eyes drifted shut. She felt his fingers slipping along her jaw, through her hair.

He was going to kiss her again…

And then what? she wondered. Where would it go from there? A summer fling? Would she sleep with him, only to become desperately attached, then they'd have to go their separate ways when the summer was over, when his therapy was finished? She'd played that game before, and all it had gotten her was a broken heart. It wasn't her that Pete wanted, he was merely looking to assert himself as a man, to feel whole again. She just happened to be the only willing and available female. And she was very easily replaceable.

She felt the whisper of his breath on her lips, felt his fingers sliding through her hair, then his lips brushed against hers…

"No!" she said it so fiercely she startled them both.

Pete dropped his hand from her hair and took a step back.

"I can't do this, doc. It's not that I don't want to. Believe me, I do. I just don't feel it would be right. It's almost like I'd be taking advantage of you."

"Maggie—"

"If the way I dress really bothers you I can run into town this afternoon and pick up some scrubs."

"You don't have to do that."

"I don't want you to be uncomfortable."

He took hold of her arms. "Maggie, it's okay. I was teasing you and it got out of hand. I'm sorry."

So what was he saying? He'd never really wanted to kiss her in the first place? That it was all just a joke?

She tried not to let it sting. Isn't that the way it had always been? She was a lot of fun in the back seat of a car, convenient to fool around with, but when it came down to relationships, guys always went for the skinny girls. The eye candy. She'd thought that would change when she lost weight. Apparently she'd been wrong.

Maybe it hadn't been her body at all, but her personality that had driven people away. Maybe the only time guys could tolerate her was when her mouth was occupied doing something other than forming words.

The idea made her sick to her stomach.

"You want me to sit back down?" he asked.

"No, I think we've both had enough of that for today. I'll grab the pails and we'll go berry picking."

He rolled his eyes. *"Again?"*

Well, he was back to his old stubborn self. How refreshing.

"Aren't they out of season yet?"

"Nope."

"How about some real therapy for a change?"

She ignored the sarcasm. "After that we need to run into town for some groceries. You're eating us out of house and home."

She saw instant wariness in his eyes.

"I think I'll hang back."

"You need to get out around people, doc. You can't hide away forever."

He started up the steps to the porch. "When I'm walking better."

"But you *are* walking better. Look how easily you just walked up those stairs. Four days ago it would have taken you twice the time."

He turned to her. "Maggie, I'm just not ready. I'm going to go throw on a shirt. Grab the pails and I'll meet you at the truck."

Maggie sighed as she watched him limp away. If only he were even half as confident physically as he was sexually. She knew he was afraid he might stumble and embarrass himself, and truthfully, that could happen. It could also happen a month from now, or six months from now. He was going to have to learn to live with that. He couldn't stay cooped up inside forever.

"If you don't come out with me soon," she called after him. "I'm going to have to do something drastic."

"Do you have any fives?"

Pete mumbled a curse and handed over his five to Maggie. "I think you're cheating."

With a smug grin, she set the pair down in her ever-growing pile on the coffee table. "Anyone ever tell you you're a poor loser?"

What did she expect? After being creamed at Connect Four, slaughtered at Aggravation, and completely sunk at Battleship, he was beginning to get a complex. He was sure with Go Fish being a game of luck, he would have a shot of winning at least a few hands.

"Do you have any queens?"

He cursed again and handed it over. "What are you, telepathic?"

She dropped the queens on her pile.

Outside, thunder rumbled and rain tinged against the aluminum awning over the porch. It had rained all afternoon and into the evening. With no television to keep them amused, and his refusal to go into town, Maggie had raided the game closet.

"This isn't fair," Pete said. "You probably played these games a million times when you were a kid, you and your sister."

"Oh, don't be such a baby. Do you have any aces?"

"Go fish."

She chose a card from the center, smiled, then set another pair down. "Your turn."

"Why is it, when I ask you about your past, you change the subject?"

Her brow tucked into a neat little frown. "I don't do that."

"Yeah, you do. When I asked if you came here a lot as a kid, you said not as much as you would have liked to. What did you mean by that?"

The frown deepened. "It's a long story."

He tossed his cards down on the table and hoisted himself up off the floor onto the couch. "Anything to circumvent another humiliating loss." He patted the couch beside him. "Come on, let's talk."

Though she didn't look thrilled with the idea, she set her cards down and circled the table to sit on the couch beside him, close enough that their thighs were just barely touching. She seemed to do that a lot—walk just close enough so that her shoulder bumped lightly against his biceps, touch his arm when she talked to him, lean over him during the therapy so that her breast would very lightly rest against his leg. Though he might have thought so at first, he was sure she didn't do it on purpose. Maybe she was just a naturally physical person. Something he'd never been. But he liked the way it made him feel. The intimacy of being physically close to another person.

He liked being close to Maggie.

"I'll talk," she said. "But first you have to tell me why you had to pay for your own college."

"Simple. I didn't want to be stuck under my father's thumb anymore. As long as he paid for my school, he controlled what classes I took, where I lived. I refused to let him run my life any longer. After the shooting, he jumped at the chance to have me back under his roof, to manipulate me again."

"So why did you go? Surely someone else could have helped you."

"Oh, no," he said. "Now it's your turn. You have to tell me why you said that about coming up here."

"Until I was fourteen, my family spent their summer vacations up here," Maggie said, looking down at her clasped hands. "I spent mine at camp."

"Why would they come up here and send you to camp?"

Somewhere deep down he could see an old wound split open and ooze bitterness.

"It was fat camp, doc. For overweight kids."

He'd heard of places like that, but he had always been under the impression they were for kids so heavy their health was at risk. "I've seen pictures of you on the wall, you didn't look that heavy to me."

"I was chubby. Not huge or anything. Actually, I was pretty small compared to a lot of the other kids, so they always kind of resented me being there. But I come from a family full of naturally thin women. Being fat wasn't acceptable."

He slid his hand down over her clenched fingers, felt her relax the slightest bit. "And traumatizing you was acceptable?"

"I think my mother believed my weight reflected on her as a parent. She really resented me for not being perfect. I used to hear her talking to her friends when she thought I wasn't around. She would say, 'Molly is my special child. She plays the piano and paints beautiful pictures and gets honors in school. Maggie just likes to eat.'"

Pete felt a sting of resentment on her behalf. "That's cruel."

"Yeah, it did wonders for my self-esteem." She said it casually, but he didn't miss the bitter undertone. He gave her hand a squeeze. "It's probably what prompted me to let Joe Murphy get all the way to third base in the backseat of his car when I was fourteen."

"Fourteen?" He hadn't even been to *first* base by then. "How old was he?"

"Seventeen. Bear in mind, I was in a D-cup bra by thirteen, so I looked a lot older than I was. And most guys saw right past the fat and focused on the breasts. Unfortunately, that's *all* they saw."

Pete had to admit, they were kind of hard to ignore. To a hormonally challenged teenaged boy they would be a beacon.

"Joe told me how beautiful I was and how much he liked me. Imagine my surprise the next day when I saw him in the hall and he had his arm around Christine D'Angelo. Who, of course, was a toothpick."

"Guys can be jerks," Pete said, feeling the need to apologize on behalf of the entire male population. "I'm sure it wasn't personal."

"Joe's best friend Dave came up to me in the hall and said he was sorry for what Joe did, that he was a real jerk. I was beautiful and nice and any guy would be lucky to go out with me. Of course I swooned, and when Dave asked if I wanted to go out with him, I practically fainted at his feet."

Pete winced, afraid he wasn't going to like what was coming next. He turned Maggie's hand over, laced his fingers through hers and she didn't stop him. Touching her, showing her that he cared was the only way he knew how to console her. "I don't think I want to hear the rest of this."

"You'd think I would have learned my lesson the first time," she said. "But that night, there I was in the back of Dave's car, and the next morning at school, he avoided me like the plague."

Pete gripped her hand tighter, shook his head with disgust.

"You would think at that point I would have caught on. But remember, I was a low self-esteem girl. Reid was next, then Mike. Finally it got back to my sister Molly what was going on and she had the extreme pleasure of informing me that all these guys had some kind of bet going to see who could get me to go all the way."

Pete mumbled a foul word under his breath.

"At this point everyone at school had heard about it, so, of course, it got back to my mother, and I went from being Maggie the fat one to Maggie the slutty one. You can probably imagine how well that went over. She said I should have known better."

It had happened years ago, when he didn't even know her. Even so it made Pete feel like putting his fist through a wall. How could anyone be that cruel? How could they use an innocent, vulnerable girl that way?

He rubbed his thumb along the edge of her palm, wishing there was something he could do, something he could say to erase the hurt in her eyes. To show her that those boys didn't matter anymore.

"My mom told me that if I ever wanted to date a nice boy I'd better lose some weight. Like, a nice boy would never date a fat girl. Maybe she thought I deserved what I got."

"I don't think I ever want to meet your mother. I'd probably end up saying something I'd regret."

Maggie shrugged and pulled her hand free, leaned forward and began gathering the cards from their abandoned game. "She did the best she could. If nothing else it toughened me up."

"That's no excuse for the way you were treated."

"No, but it's just the way things are." Maggie yawned and looked at her watch. "I didn't realize how late it is. I'm beat."

It was barely nine-thirty, but Maggie usually went to bed around ten, if not earlier. Not unusual considering she was up at the crack of dawn exercising. It was no wonder she ate like a bird and worked out so much. Those boys had humiliated her, her mother had shattered her self-esteem. And he was guessing he probably hadn't heard everything. What other horrible things had Maggie dealt with growing up?

He wasn't sure he wanted to know.

"We have a long day ahead of us tomorrow, so make sure you get a good night's sleep," she told him, rising from the couch.

He grabbed her hand again. "I know you probably won't believe this, but it wouldn't have mattered to me."

"What wouldn't have mattered?"

"Your weight. It's what's on the inside that counts."

She gazed down at their hands linked together and only looked sadder. More lonely. "I'll bet you told yourself that very same thing while you were slaving away in the weight room." She gave him a look, one that said he was full of it, then she pulled her hand free and walked to her bedroom, shutting the door behind her.

He had no reason to feel guilty, to feel as if he'd wronged her somehow, but he did anyway.

Eight

*P*ete raised his hand to press the elevator button when he heard a loud pop from the direction of the ER.

It's happening again, he thought. I have to stop it this time.

People were running past him, knocking him from side to side, their faces masks of terror.

Rachel. He had to get to Rachel.

He fought his way back toward triage. More gunshots rang out, more screaming. He tried to run faster, but his legs felt as if they'd been encased in cement. If he could just get there sooner he might be able to save her this time.

He rounded the corner, saw Rachel lying facedown in the hallway.

"No!"

His world shifted into slow motion as he started down the hall toward her, barely aware of the gunfire. His only concern, *as blood began to pool around her midsection, was getting her out of that hallway. He racked his brain to remember her blood type.*

He heard another pop. Then another, closer this time, then a third and a fourth, and pain seared him like a red-hot brand through his chest, knocking him off balance. Another pop and he felt the sickening thud of bullet to bone, felt the flesh of his knee as it was torn away. His leg gave out and he crumpled like a rag doll, his cheek smashing hard against the cold floor. Pain such as he'd never imagined possible slammed the air from his lungs. He squeezed his eyes shut, forcing down the bile filling his throat. Rachel was only inches away, if he could just….

He lifted his arms, tried to pull himself across the floor, and saw that his left hand was soaked with blood. His blood. The pain was all-encompassing, making him dizzy and limp. He struggled for breath and realized his lung must have been pierced. He was going to die right there on the floor before he could help Rachel.

Feeling himself slipping into unconsciousness, he forced his eyes open. He was going to Florida tomorrow to teach his fiancée to water-ski. He was going to get married and have a family—he had plans, damn it. He couldn't die, not like this, not without a fight. Closing his eyes in concentration, he thrust his hand out, stretching until he felt the cotton of Rachel's scrubs. Clasping at the fabric, he pulled himself closer, fumbling to feel for a pulse at the base of her throat. Nothing. He tried to pull himself closer, to stop the bleeding, but he couldn't make his arms move. His eyes drifted closed again and his head dropped onto the floor.

Then he heard shouting. It was fuzzy, but close. He felt hands on his arms and legs, recognized the pressure being applied to his wounds, felt himself being lifted. He saw lights and movement through bleary eyes.

"She's gone," he heard someone say, and forced his eyes open, looking down at his colleague—his best friend—still sprawled on the floor. Eyes cold and hollow and lifeless.

"No," he moaned, closing his eyes. He hadn't been able to save her. He'd failed her again.

"Doc."

"Hang in there, Pete," someone was urging. "You're going to be okay. Keep fighting."

"Doc."

He didn't want to live. He just wanted to die, he wanted it to be over with. The pain was too intense, too deep. But someone was shaking him—

"Pete, wake up!"

Pete gasped in a breath and shot up in bed, heart slamming against his ribcage, bile rising in his throat, choking him. Blackness surrounded him and for a second he didn't know where he was, or if the hands rubbing his back, the calm voice soothing him, were part of the dream or just a figment of his imagination.

"It's okay. It was just a dream."

Then he realized, it was Maggie's voice, Maggie's hands. As his vision cleared and his eyes adjusted to the dark, he saw her silhouette crouched beside him on the bed. Her arms went around him, her sweet scent erasing the bitter metallic stench of blood still haunting him.

"I couldn't save her," he said, tears stinging his eyes. "I let her die."

"Shhh." Maggie rocked him gently. "It's okay. It's over."

But it wasn't over, not as long as he kept reliving it again and again in his sleep. It would never be over. "I didn't get to her fast enough. I had to lie there and watch her die."

She leaned back against the headboard, easing him down with her. "Lie down, try to go back to sleep."

Exhausted, he curled up beside her, head in her lap, shivering as the fan across the room blew cool air over his damp skin. Maggie reached down and untangled the sheet from his legs, covering him with it. He was too damned cold, too sick in his soul to care that she was seeing him this way—even to care that he was naked.

He only cared that he wasn't alone.

"Relax," Maggie said, gently stroking the hair back from his forehead. "Go back to sleep."

His lids began to feel heavy, so he let his eyes drift closed. He wrapped an arm around her waist, pulling himself closer, absorbing her heat.

With Maggie's hands soothing him, her gentle voice lulling him, he slipped into a deep, dreamless sleep.

Pete opened his eyes, but when he reached for Maggie, he found himself hugging a pillow instead. He would have thought it was all a dream if not for her scent still clinging to the pillowcase, the form of her body pressed into the sheets beside him. The air was thick with humidity from last night's rain and the sheet clung to his skin. It was going to be another unbearably hot day.

He glanced over at the clock and saw that it was after eight, meaning Maggie was probably out for her morning run. At least he'd have a minute or two to pull himself together before he had to face her. He could only imagine what she would think of him after the way he'd behaved last night. At least he'd managed not to throw up this time, and he hadn't woken wracked with sobs as he had so many times that first month he was out of the hospital.

When the dreams had gradually tapered off, he'd thought he'd seen the last of them. Working with Maggie, being forced to deal with this on a daily basis, was dredging it all up again. It seemed as though whenever he tried to get on with his life, to put the shooting behind him, something kept dragging him back down, forcing him to relive it.

From the other room he heard the squeak of the porch door opening and footsteps on the creaky wood floor. Maggie was back. He heard the fridge open as she got herself a bottle of water, then a loud thump, as if maybe she'd closed a cupboard door.

Could it be possible that she was actually cleaning up after herself? Wouldn't that be a novelty? he thought with a wry smile. Cleanliness wasn't exactly one of her strong suits. Every morning he came out to find the remains of her breakfast waiting for him on the kitchen counter, and she never picked up her wet towel from the bathroom floor after she took a shower. Not to mention she usually left her clothes discarded there, too, and her shoes all over the house for him to trip on. He was constantly stuffing her clothes in the hamper and dropping her shoes by the back door. She never cleaned up when she made a meal either, and since dirty dishes in the sink grated on his nerves, he usually cleaned that up, too.

It all seemed trivial when he thought about everything

she'd been through, and all she'd done for him. The way she'd been there for him last night.

He swung his legs over the edge of the bed and sat up. No point in trying to put off the inevitable. He was going to have to apologize for last night, and try to figure out some way to explain what had happened—without her thinking he was a big wuss.

He got dressed and brushed his teeth, then headed out to the kitchen, confused at first to find the refrigerator door hanging open, until he looked down and saw Maggie lying on the kitchen floor, out cold. She looked peaceful, as if she'd just decided to plop down and take a nap. It took a full ten seconds for the reality of what he was seeing to kick in—pretty pathetic for an ER doctor. The thump he'd heard hadn't been a cabinet door closing, it had been Maggie hitting the floor.

As fast as his legs would carry him, he was at her side. Ignoring the ache in his knee, he lowered himself to the floor and knelt beside her. "Maggie, wake up."

When she didn't open her eyes a slug of fear lodged itself in his gut. Sweat soaked her clothes, her skin was clammy and deathly pale, and she had dark smudges under her eyes. He pressed two fingers to the inside of her wrist, wishing he'd brought a stethoscope and blood pressure cuff with him. "Maggie, can you hear me?"

He grabbed the bottle of water from the floor beside her and poured some into his hand then patted her cheeks. "Come on, Maggie, wake up."

Her eyes fluttered open, she gazed blearily up, and for a second he didn't think she was really seeing him. Then she blinked a few times, and recognition seemed to set in—then confusion.

"Hey, doc. Why am I lying on the floor?"

"My guess is that you're dehydrated and you've pushed yourself too hard on too little food. But I'm going to want a second opinion on that. Can you sit up?"

"I think so."

"Take it slow," he said, taking her hand and helping her. She swayed halfway up, clutching his arm to steady herself. "Easy."

When she was upright and steady, he handed her the water. "Drink this slowly."

She took small sips of the water. Already the color was returning to her cheeks, but she still looked like hell.

"Have you ever passed out before?"

She shook her head. "Nope, this is new for me."

"But you've been dizzy lately?"

"Sometimes, but it's probably just from the heat."

"Nausea?"

"Also from the heat."

"Missed periods?"

She shot him a scathing look. "You have to have sex to get pregnant, doc."

"You can miss periods for a lot of reasons other than pregnancy."

"No, I haven't missed any periods. Not completely."

"But you've been irregular?"

"A little."

"How little?"

She frowned. "I don't know that I'm comfortable having this conversation with you."

"I'm a doctor, Maggie. How irregular?"

"Last month I just spotted."

Pete slowly rose, gripping the edge of the counter to pull himself to his feet. "Where are your car keys?"

"Why?"

"You said you would do something drastic if I didn't go to town with you. I guess you weren't kidding."

"You think I did this on *purpose?*"

"Your keys?"

"In the bedroom. Where are we going?"

"I'm taking you to the hospital."

She shook her head. "No way. I'm okay, doc."

"No, you're not. You're dehydrated, malnourished and I'm guessing you're probably anemic."

"I feel fine." To illustrate her point, she pulled herself to her feet…and lost her balance on the way up. If Pete hadn't been there to grab hold of her she would have wound up right back on her butt on the kitchen floor.

"No arguments," he said when she opened her mouth to plead her case. "You're going."

"Your blood pressure is low, you're dehydrated and though I won't know for sure until we get the results of your blood tests back, you're most likely anemic."

Pete shot Maggie an I-told-you-so look.

She stuck her tongue out at him.

Dr. Cartwright, who looked to be about the same age as Pete—and was almost as cute in a preppy sort of way—gave them an odd look. He had run down a laundry list of about a million questions, and spent the last fifteen minutes poking and prodding her.

"I'll get you started on an iron supplement, but the best way to keep your iron levels up is through a balanced diet."

"That could be a problem considering she never eats," Pete said, and Maggie glared at him.

"I do so. I eat three meals a day."

"What's your typical daily intake?" the doctor asked.

Maggie faltered, knowing it was going to sound like a lot less than it really was. To lose those last five pounds, she needed to keep her calorie intake low and her activity level high.

"She eats cottage cheese and fruit for breakfast," Pete said for her. "A diet shake for lunch and usually a salad for dinner."

The doctor regarded her with a lifted brow. "Does that sound about right?"

"And she works out vigorously for about two hours a day," Pete added.

Maggie shot him another scathing look. He was making it sound a lot worse than it was. "I'm trying to lose the last five pounds and I hit a plateau so I cut my calorie intake," she explained to the doctor. "As soon as I lose the weight, I'll eat more."

"What do you weigh now?" he asked.

Maggie chewed the inside of her cheek. "I'm not sure exactly. The cottage doesn't have a scale. But my clothes haven't gotten too much looser."

"How can you tell?" Pete asked. "Everything you own is a size too small."

Oh, he was really asking for it now. So she liked her clothes snug, big deal. Was that a crime? He didn't seem to mind so much when he was ogling her breasts.

"Why don't we take a trip to the scale?" Dr. Cartwright suggested, sliding back the curtain. Maggie hopped down from the bed and followed him, holding her gown closed so her rear end didn't hang out. Pete trailed behind them.

Maggie climbed onto the scale and Pete watched over her shoulder as the doctor slid the weights over. She expected him to stop at one-thirty, where she'd been stuck for the past month, but that didn't balance the scale. She watched, stunned as he tapped the weight all the way down to one-fifteen.

One hundred and fifteen? How was that possible?

She shook her head. "That can't be right."

"These scales are calibrated monthly. It's right."

Why didn't she feel thin? How could she be ten pounds *under* her goal weight and still feel fat?

"This can't be right," she insisted. "It has to be wrong."

"It's not wrong," Pete said from behind her.

"A woman your age, with your frame, should weigh between one-twenty-five and one-thirty-five," the doctor said. "You're about ten pounds underweight."

Maggie stepped down from the scale. "So why don't I feel thin?"

Pete and the doctor exchanged a look, and Maggie knew exactly what they were thinking, but they were wrong.

"Don't even look at me like that. I do not have an eating disorder."

"Let's go back in the exam room," Dr. Cartwright said. When they were there he pulled the curtain closed. "I know you don't want to hear this, Mrs.—"

"Ms.," Maggie corrected. "I'm not married."

He looked questioningly at Pete.

"He's my patient," she said. "I'm a physical therapist."

The doctor nodded, but still looked as though he didn't get

it. "I know you won't want to hear this, but you're making yourself sick. You need to start eating a healthy diet or you run the risk of severe health problems. The worst being heart failure."

"No more of this diet crap," Pete said, and the ferocity with which he spoke startled her. He sounded…worried. *Really* worried. "You're going to start eating balanced meals until we get your weight back up." He turned to Dr Cartwright. "Any possibility you might have a spare blood pressure cuff lying around I could borrow for a while?"

"I could probably scrounge one up. You know how to use it?"

"I'm a doctor—emergency medicine," Pete said, and held up the cane. "Medical leave. I'm recovering from an…accident."

"Where do you work?"

"Henry Ford Hospital in Detroit. We both do," he said, nodding to Maggie.

"I know of it. They had that terrible shooting earlier this year. One doctor killed, another one…" He trailed off when he saw the tight look on Pete's face. "You weren't…?"

Pete shifted uncomfortably, leaning on his cane. "Yeah, that would be me."

An awkward silence followed. What did you say to something like that? *Sorry* just didn't cut it. This was exactly the kind of thing Pete didn't want to deal with, and the very thing he would have to learn to.

"Jeremy Cartwright," the doctor finally said, shaking Pete's hand.

"Pete Morgan."

"How long are you two planning on being in town?"

"Through the summer," Pete said.

"If you're up to it physically, and you can spare a few hours a week, there's a free clinic in Alma, about thirty miles from here. We're desperate for volunteers. It's not going to be as fast-paced as an urban ER—mostly ear infections, poison ivy, allergic reactions, things like that. But it's for a good cause."

For a second Pete looked interested, then something dark passed over his eyes. "I'm not sure if I would have time with my therapy."

He wanted to do it, Maggie was sure of it. In his heart, he would always be a doctor, whether he was practicing or not. The desire to help people wasn't one that went away.

This might be just the thing he needed to bring him around.

"We can adjust your therapy schedule," she said. She didn't want to push, but this was too good an opportunity to pass up. He *needed* to do this—even if he didn't realize it.

And now she had leverage.

"We have openings in pretty much every shift, so you would be free to make your own hours. And we're never short on patients." Jeremy jotted a few numbers down on a piece of paper and handed it to Pete. "Here's my beeper and home number. If you change your mind, call me."

"Could you excuse us for a minute, doc?" Maggie asked Pete. "I need a couple of minutes alone with the doctor."

Pete regarded her suspiciously.

"Female stuff," she said.

He nodded, but she could tell he didn't believe her. "I'll wait for you outside."

He left, and Maggie peeked out the curtain, to be sure that he wasn't lurking outside eavesdropping. When she turned back around, Jeremy was grinning.

"I'm guessing there's no female issue."

She shook her head.

"How bad was it? His injuries, I mean."

"Bad. He was shot twice in the chest and once in the knee. He's lucky to be alive."

"And the other doctor?"

"Killed instantly. Witnesses said that when Pete saw her lying there, he just started running toward her. He didn't even notice there was a kid with a gun standing at the end of the hall. All he cared about was trying to save her."

"It's normal to see gunshot wounds in the ER, maybe not so much here. But when it's one of your own…" He shook his head. "He seems to be getting around pretty well though."

"Most of his problem now is accepting his disability. He thinks he can't have a career in medicine because he can't keep up with the fast pace of the ER. I think working in the clinic will help him realize that he's capable of a lot more than he thinks. He needs to take this volunteer position. I want to incorporate it into his therapy."

"I'll be happy to help out any way I can, but I can't force him."

"You won't have to." A devious smile curled her mouth. "If I've learned one thing as a therapist, it's how to be persuasive."

Nine

Maggie walked out to the emergency center parking lot and found Pete leaning against the back of her SUV, arms folded over his chest, a grim look on his face.

Despite that, he looked good. Better than he had living in that tomb in his parents' house. He looked…healthy. His hair was still on the long side, but he'd lost that pasty white pallor. His skin was deeply tanned from all the long walks they'd been taking and he spent a lot of time in the afternoons on the beach doing sit-ups and push-ups, trying to maintain his upper-body strength.

He was nowhere close to having the muscle mass he'd had before the shooting, but he looked healthy and happy, and in her book, that was all that mattered.

Pete jingled her keys from his finger. "You okay to drive?"

"Actually, I'm still feeling a little woozy," she lied. "You can drive."

He opened her door for her, then walked around and got in on the driver's side. He set his cane on the floor. "Things are going to change around the cottage," he said.

She fastened her seatbelt. "Oh, yeah? What things?"

He started the engine and put the SUV into gear, backing out from the space and driving toward the exit. "Until your blood pressure is up and your iron levels are higher, you can forget about exercising."

Dr. Cartwright had said as much, but hearing it from Pete was entirely different. He wasn't her doctor. It made her feel rebellious. "Says who?"

"Says me."

"I have two words for you," she said. *"Bite me."*

"I'm serious, Maggie. You're going to start taking care of yourself." He pulled out into traffic, but in the opposite direction from the lake.

"You're going the wrong way, Einstein. Home is in the other direction."

"We're not going home. We're going shopping."

"We are? Mr. I'm-just-not-ready-to-go-out?"

"We need supplies," he said. "And I can't trust you to make the trip alone."

"Oh, that reminds me." She pulled the blood pressure cuff from her bag and tossed it at him. "Jeremy asked me to give that to you."

He set it on the seat between them. "We also need a scale. And more food."

Well, she'd wanted to get him out of the house and around people. And here they were. And she knew for a fact he hadn't driven since the shooting, so that was a step forward, too.

So why did she have a sinking feeling in her stomach?

"What kind of food?"

"Chicken, fish, beef. Foods rich in iron. We're going to weigh you daily until you're back up to where you should be."

The thought of eating meat was only slightly more offensive than the reality of hopping on a scale every day. "And if I refuse?"

"Not an option. I'll force-feed you if I have to." He pulled into the Carter's parking lot and swung into a spot. "Don't think I won't do it."

Oh, she would never make that mistake. Pete was a man of his word.

And then some.

He grabbed his cane, opened his door and lowered himself down. She hopped out and met him around back. Concern she understood, but he was being downright bossy.

"Why do you even care, doc? I'm not your patient." He started to walk around her and she stepped in his way. "What difference does it make how much I weigh?"

"Don't push me, Maggie," he said tightly. "I'm not in the mood."

He wasn't concerned, he was *angry* with her.

Her own anger sparked. "Do you really think getting mad at me is going to make this any easier?"

He grabbed her upper arm and backed her against the tail of the SUV. "What makes me mad," he said through gritted teeth, "is those jerks, for the way they treated you back in high school, and your mother, for making you feel inadequate for what was obviously her own damned neurosis."

Something dark and dangerous flared in his eyes. His gaze drifted lower, to her mouth, lingering there.

He was going to kiss her again. And the crazy thing was, she *wanted* him to, even though she knew it was wrong.

His head dipped lower, his eyes still on her mouth, and her lips felt warm and full. So ready to take whatever he offered. He held himself there for a second, as if he couldn't decide whether he really wanted to do it. Then he cursed under his breath, lowered his head, and crushed his lips against hers. This was no sweet, seductive kiss. This was a bruising, punishing kiss. She couldn't help wondering who it was exactly he was trying to punish—her or himself. She only knew there was more passion, more emotion in that simple gesture than in the last fifty times she'd been kissed. Her heart dropped to the pit of her stomach, her knees went rubbery and flames ignited in her soul.

He ended the kiss as abruptly as he'd begun it, and backed away just far enough to look her in the eyes. "Now, we're going in that store, and we're buying food, then we're going to find a medical supply store and we're going to get a scale. And you'll eat what I tell you to, and you'll get on the scale every damned morning until I say you can stop. Understand?"

Something told her now was not the time to argue, so she gave him a wobbly nod.

He let go of her arm. "That's more like it. Now let's get this over with."

He backed away and her knees were so weak and her head so swimmy she nearly slid down the back hatch and hit the pavement.

What was that?

She knew he found her attractive, and probably even liked

her a little, misguided as he was. But this concern for her health, for the way she'd been treated…she was stunned. If she didn't know any better she might think—

No, she wouldn't even let herself think that, because it would never happen. She wouldn't *let* it happen. It wasn't uncommon for patients to develop close relationships with their therapists. With her and Pete living together, being so close in every respect, and being two healthy—well, relatively healthy—adults, emotions were bound to be blown way out of proportion.

She'd seen it before, and she'd made some really lousy judgment calls.

She wouldn't be doing that again.

Maggie sat at the table, twisting her napkin in her lap, staring at her plate. Pete had made grilled salmon fillets topped with a butter-dill sauce and served them with steamed broccoli and seasoned brown rice. She mentally calculated how many zillions of calories were sitting on her plate and her stomach heaved.

"Dig in," he said. "You're not leaving this table until your plate is clean."

"Whatever you say, *Dad*."

The insult rolled off his back. "Don't think you're going to sass your way out of this one, Maggie. I'm serious."

Which fit right in with her plan. It was time for the bargaining to begin. She took a deep breath and blew it out. "I'll eat this, but only on one condition."

His fork stopped halfway to his mouth. "What condition?"

"You have to agree to volunteer at the clinic."

He frowned and put down his fork. "You know how I feel about that."

"And you know how I feel about eating, but you're forcing me to do it anyway."

"Because not eating is unhealthy."

"Hiding yourself away from the world isn't healthy either, doc. You went out today, and did you have a problem? Did anyone point and laugh? Did you fall, or even stumble?"

He only stared at her.

"All I'm asking for is a couple of hours a day, twice a week. It'll be part of your therapy. Give it two weeks and if you really hate it, you can stop."

"And if I say no?"

She pushed her plate away. "You're eating alone."

"It's only been eleven days."

"And you're doing great, doc. You're ready for this." She pulled Jeremy's number from her back pocket. She gave him that and her cell phone. "Make the call."

For a full minute he only looked at her outstretched hand. Finally he took the phone and the number and dialed. "Jeremy, this is Pete Morgan. I'd like to take you up on that volunteer position." Pete nodded toward her plate.

Maggie pulled it back in front of her and picked up her fork.

"I was thinking two days a week to start."

She broke off a small bite of fish and lifted it to her mouth. She glanced up at Pete and he nodded.

"Tuesday and Thursday afternoons would be great."

Before she could talk herself out of it, or stop to think about the calories she would be ingesting and the rolls of fat she'd worked so hard to shed, Maggie closed her eyes and shoved the fork in her mouth. Her taste buds went into overdrive as the tangy sauce hit her tongue. The flavor was so intense she nearly gagged.

Instead, she forced herself to chew very slowly, then swallow.

"Eleven to four would be fine," Pete was saying, his eyes not leaving her face. He gave her another nod, as if to say, take another bite.

She loaded her fork with rice and her mouth actually watered in anticipation. The rice was spicy and cooked just right. It had been so long since she'd had real food, she'd forgotten how much she used to love to eat. It scared the heck out of her because it would be so easy to fall back into her old habits. So easy to become fat Maggie again.

"I don't know, let me ask," Pete said, then asked Maggie, "Do I need directions to the clinic?"

"I know where it is."

"Nope," he told Jeremy, "I'm good."

Maggie tried her broccoli next. It was seasoned with lemon juice and what tasted like garlic salt, so it couldn't have too many calories. And it was delicious.

"She's good," Pete said with another pointed look her way. "She's eating dinner right now." He laughed, then said, "Yeah, she is."

Maggie narrowed her eyes at him.

"Sounds good. I'll see you Tuesday." He snapped her phone closed and set it on the table.

"Yeah, I am what?" she asked.

"He asked if you were giving me any trouble about the eating. How is it, by the way?"

"Wonderful," she said, taking another bite of her fish. "Where did you learn to cook?"

He shrugged. "Here and there. When you're a bachelor, especially one with a crazy schedule, you either learn to cook, or you eat a lot of fast food."

"I never learned to cook, and I ate nothing but fast food for a long time. Which explains why I looked the way I did, I guess."

"I think genetics has a lot to do with it, too. I know for me it does. But it's always better for you in the long run to eat healthily." He looked up at her and grinned. "That's the doctor in me talking."

"Maybe you should do most of the cooking from now on," she said, "since you're so much better at it than I am."

"I'll cook if you do the dishes. And I mean *after* dinner, not the next morning."

"Dirty dishes really drive you nuts, don't they?"

"So do dirty clothes and wet towels strewn all over the bathroom floor. And shoes left in the middle of the room where I inevitably trip on them."

"I don't leave my shoes in the middle of the room. I take them off by the back door."

Pete nodded in the direction of the couch, and she turned to see her flip-flops lying there, in the middle of the floor, right where she'd kicked them off. "Oops."

"I'm the one who puts your shoes by the back door," he said. "You leave them all over the place."

"I'll try not to do that," she said.

"I would appreciate it."

"I'll try to remember to put my dirty clothes and towels in

the hamper, too." She pushed her rice around with her fork, working up the will to take another bite. "Despite all the little stuff, I think this is working out pretty well. I mean, we seem to get along okay."

"Yeah, we do," he agreed.

"When you're not being bossy and overbearing," she added.

He gave her a wry smile. "Yeah, because we both know you don't have a bossy bone in your body."

She smiled. The truth was, she liked that he kept her on her toes. It made life interesting. She'd never had a roommate like Pete before. And while she'd had lots of male friends over the years, there was something more than that with him.

Something...*special.*

He took a bite of fish, chewing slowly, eyes fixed on his plate. "By the way, I wanted to um, talk to you about last night."

She forced herself to take another bite. "What about it?"

"I wanted to apologize."

Chew...chew...swallow. "What for?"

"For waking you. For making you feel like you had to stay with me."

She'd kind of expected him to be embarrassed about the nightmare. It probably made him feel weak, and, like most men she knew, Pete hated feeling weak.

She took another bite. "Do you have nightmares a lot?"

"At first I did. Almost every night. They stopped after a couple of months. Now they're back."

Bite. Chew...chew...swallow. "Did it help having me there?"

"Yeah, it did, but—"

"Then don't worry about it. I didn't mind." Bite. Chew... chew...swallow. If she thought of eating as a process, and forgot about the ramifications, it was a little easier to do. "Out of curiosity, have you ever talked to anyone about it?"

"About my dreams?"

"No, about the shooting."

He shrugged. "What's to talk about? It happened, now it's over. I've dealt with it."

"Have you really?"

"Don't psychoanalyze me, Maggie."

"It was only a suggestion. Just know that I'm here to talk if you need to."

They ate in silence for several minutes, until Maggie's plate was nearly empty. And she felt full. She couldn't remember the last time she'd eaten until she was satisfied. But instead of satisfied, she began to feel edgy and panicked, like she'd just done something reprehensible. Like she needed to get the food out of her body, before it broke down and turned into fat. She could practically feel the fat cells forming and sticking to her insides. The waist of her shorts felt too tight and her top stretched snugly over her stomach.

Pete had piled twice the amount of food she'd had on his plate and had eaten every bite, down to the last grain of rice, but he wouldn't be gaining any weight.

It was so unfair.

What was wrong with being a little underweight, anyway? Maybe if she promised not to lose any more weight they would let her stay the way she was. How bad could it be really? There were lots of skinny people in the world.

The panic multiplied. Her stomach clutched, feeling

bloated and overfull. Sweat popped out on her brow and she felt nauseated. She glanced in the direction of the bathroom. Would it really hurt, just this once…?

"Don't even think about it," Pete said sharply and Maggie jumped at the sound of his voice.

"Th-think about what?"

"Losing your dinner. It's not going to happen, so just forget it."

She made an indignant noise. "Now you think I'm bulimic?"

"All I know is that you look like you're about to crawl out of your skin, and you keep glancing in the direction of the bathroom. But I won't let you do it. If I have to duct-tape your mouth shut, I will."

She resented the implication, but what bothered her even more, what had fear gripping her, was that he was right. She *was* actually considering making herself throw up. Suppose she did do it this one time. What would stop her from doing it a second time and a third?

"I've seen first-hand what happens to women who binge and purge, Maggie. Trust me when I say, it's not a pretty sight. It's a control issue. And once you start, it's nearly impossible to stop, not without intensive therapy. Is that what you want?"

She sucked in an unsteady breath and clasped her hands together to keep them from shaking. He was right, she wasn't used to this feeling of helplessness. She might have made her share of mistakes, but she'd always been in control of her life. She felt as if that had suddenly been snatched away.

"You'll get through this," Pete said. There was so much compassion in his eyes it made her go all mushy inside. He leaned across the table and put a hand over both of hers. "We both will."

The fact that she wasn't in this alone, that in a small way he understood what she was going through, made it a little less scary. She wondered what might have happened if Pete hadn't been there to boss her around. Would she have had the ability to see what she was doing to herself, or would she have just kept losing weight until there was nothing left of her?

Ten

Maggie flopped on her stomach, driving her fists into the pillow in a fit of pure frustration. This was the fourth night since Pete had taken her to the hospital that she couldn't sleep. The fourth night she'd tossed and turned until she felt like screaming and banging her head against the wall. She wasn't sure if it was the sudden lack of activity or the abnormally high calorie intake or the fact that she felt as though her life was spinning out of control. Whatever it was, it was driving her crazy.

She heard a noise from the other room and pushed herself up on her elbows to listen. Pete hadn't had a nightmare in days. He'd begun work at the clinic on Tuesday, as promised. After his shift, when he got home, she'd asked him how it went and he gave her a noncommittal shrug. She hadn't pushed. She knew when he was ready to talk about it he would.

Sure enough, during dinner, as she forced herself to choke down a grilled chicken breast and a baked potato, he mentioned how swamped he'd been with patients.

"You wouldn't believe how many people can't afford decent health care," he'd said. "Without the clinic these people would have no place else to go. I had a little boy in today suffering from recurring ear infections. He's had so many he has significant hearing loss."

"Can you help him?"

"He needs a myringotomy. It's a simple out-patient procedure, but his parents don't have health insurance. Without insurance it could cost thousands. His mother said her husband was laid off and they're barely making ends meet as it is. They just can't afford it."

"What about public assistance?" she'd asked.

"She makes enough money that they don't qualify. In the ER we treat everyone, whether they have insurance or not, so I never really considered the effect a lack of insurance would have for non-emergency health care."

"So, what you're doing there is good?"

He nodded. "Yeah, I guess it is."

That afternoon after work he'd told her about the other doctors who worked there and a few of his more interesting cases. "It's kind of a challenge," he said. "Trying to figure out the best and cheapest way to treat people. And the gratitude in their eyes...I feel like I'm really making a difference."

"You are, doc," she had told him, and he'd smiled. For the first time since they'd come here she could finally see the light at the end of the tunnel. She had real hope that Pete was beginning to accept his disability and his limitations.

Herself, now, that was another story altogether.

Maggie lowered her head back down on the pillow and closed her eyes, then she heard the noise again.

"Rachel, no!"

Oh, damn, Pete was having another nightmare.

She scrambled out of bed and darted across the hall. She didn't turn on the light this time, knowing she would get an eyeful if she did. And sure enough, as she stepped closer to the bed she could see that Pete was sprawled out, only half-covered by the sheet. She couldn't see a lot in the dark, but she could see enough to know that he was naked. Even with Pete in this distressed state, she wasn't immune to all that lean muscle and tanned skin.

His head thrashed across the pillow and he moaned in his sleep. She slipped into bed beside him, grabbed his shoulder, and gave it a shake. His skin was hot and slippery with perspiration. "Doc, wake up. You're having a bad dream."

He moaned and grimaced in his sleep.

"Pete, wake up!"

As he had the first time, Pete shot up in bed, his breath coming hard and fast.

"It's okay," she said softly, smoothing her hands down his back. "It was just a dream."

He looked dazedly around, as if he wasn't sure where he was. Then he blinked a few times and asked in a raspy voice, "What time is it?"

She combed her fingers through his damp hair. "Two o'clock."

"I woke you again," he said, dragging a hand over his face.

"It's okay. I was already awake." She eased him back against the pillows. "Lie down, relax."

"Are you leaving?" There was a note of panic in his voice that made her smile. He wouldn't ask her to stay, he was too proud for that. Too macho. But he wanted her to.

"I'm not going anywhere." She scooted down beside him and he shifted closer, wrapping his arm around her waist and resting his head on her shoulder. She enjoyed this far too much for her own good. The sheet was tangled around his legs and she did her best to keep her eyes from wandering south. If this became a habit, the man was going to have to think about wearing pajamas to bed. A girl could only take so much of that body before her thoughts turned wicked.

She was already ninety percent there.

"You don't have to stay," he said, though he had an awfully tight grip on her. His breath was warm against her neck, the hand wrapped around her waist so large and sure.

Things had been so uncertain for her lately, but here, lying with Pete, she felt...safe. Maybe she needed this as much as he did.

"I'm staying," she said.

"I'm naked, you know."

"I know."

"That doesn't bother you?"

"I have my eyes closed."

He paused then asked, "Do you really?"

"No, not really."

He chuckled lightly, and she knew he was feeling better. "Like you said, if you've seen one you've seen them all, huh?"

"Don't forget, I've seen *yours*."

He was quiet for a second, then said, "That's a little unfair, don't you think?"

"What is?"

"That you've seen mine. To make it fair, you should show me yours."

Oh yeah, like that would ever happen. "Who ever said life is fair, doc?"

He gripped her nightshirt, gathering the fabric in his hand, easing it up over her thighs. "Just one little peek…"

She didn't make a move to stop him, positive he was bluffing, or at the very least just trying to annoy her. And maybe a small part of her was intrigued by the idea of a little show and tell—until her shirt was up to her waist and he hooked his fingers in the top of her panties, lifting his head like he was really going to take a peek. Then she smacked his hand. Hard.

"Ow!" he said, yanking his hand back, but she could hear a smile in his voice. "Jeez, you're mean."

She tugged her nightshirt back down. "Try that again and you're liable to lose that hand."

"Yeah, but it would be worth it," he said, and the comment warmed her all over. If he was only saying it to be nice, to make her feel good, it had worked. That charm could play dangerous games with her head.

He was quiet for a minute then asked, "Do you think this is weird? Us sleeping together? I'm assuming you don't do this with your other patients."

She laughed softly. "No, this isn't usually part of the therapy. Of course, I don't move in with my other patients either. So, yes, I guess you could say the entire arrangement is a little weird."

"We've definitely transcended the typical therapist-patient relationship."

"Definitely."

"I think what we have is a lot more than a friendship, too."

"I do, too."

"You do know how much I care about you?"

Not as much as I care about you, she wanted to say. Too much to be anything but friends. "I care about you, too," she said.

He settled his head back against her shoulder. "Maggie, why don't you have a boyfriend?"

"Why do you want to know?"

"Just curious."

"I had a...bad experience."

"With a boyfriend?"

"He was sort of my fiancé."

He rose up on one elbow and gazed at her through the dark. "This isn't one of those stories that's going to make me feel like punching something, is it?"

"He was a patient."

"I thought you don't get involved with patients."

"Normally no, and it wasn't the first time one had a thing for me, but I really thought it was different with this guy. He really seemed to care about me."

"And..."

"And I was wrong." Yet another failure in the ever-growing list her mother had been keeping since Maggie had left the womb.

When she'd started dating her ex, her mother had been ecstatic. He was attractive, successful—the perfect man in her mother's eyes. When he'd asked Maggie to marry him, her parents had been over the moon with joy, and Maggie finally felt as if she had done something right, she'd pleased them—until her mother threw in a little disclaimer.

"You finally have a chance at real happiness," she told Maggie. "*Don't* blow this."

As if the relationship had been destined to fail otherwise. And maybe it had been. Maybe she was really that unlovable, that undesirable.

Telling her parents the wedding was off, that she'd been unceremoniously dumped, had been the most humiliating thing she'd ever had to do. And of course her mother saw it as another failure. Instead of drawing Maggie into her arms and soothing her, she'd berated her.

"I should have known," her mother had said, shaking her head. "I swear, Maggie, you do this on purpose just to hurt me."

Once again, she'd made it all about herself, how *she* felt. That had been the final straw for Maggie. It was the moment she realized that her mother didn't care about her feelings and probably never would.

"What happened?" Pete asked.

"He met someone else," she said. Someone thin and delicate and submissive.

You're so bossy, he used to tell her. *Do you always have to be right?* And he would nag her constantly about her weight. It was her mother all over again.

But she'd stayed with him. It was that or disappoint her parents. However, she'd discovered, there were worse things than making her mother unhappy. Being stuck in a relationship with a man who would have made her miserable, who would have constantly fed her low self-esteem—that would have been the ultimate mistake.

When she got over the hurt and realized how much better off she was, she was grateful he'd dumped her. She never would have had the courage to end it herself. And it had taught her an important lesson. Good things, happy relationships, didn't happen to people like her.

There was a long stretch of silence, then Pete said, "You know I would never hurt you, Maggie."

"People don't usually go into a relationship intending to hurt someone," she said. "But they still do."

"I like being with you. You're so different from anyone I've been attracted to before."

"You're in limbo, doc. Right now a lot of your world revolves around me. It's normal to form attachments. When you've finished your therapy, the feeling will fade. Trust me."

"You don't know that."

"Yes," she said, with a finality that shot a dagger of pain through his heart. "I do."

Pete woke with his hand cupped around something soft and warm. He didn't have to open his eyes to know it was still dark or that the warm body curled up beside him was Maggie. She lay in the crook of his body, pressed tightly against him, her head resting on his other arm, her cute little behind tucked intimately against his crotch with only a very thin pair of panties in between. He could feel her nightshirt bunched around her waist and the backs of her bare legs against his upper thighs. The soft thing in his hand was her breast, and he was more than a little aroused.

Well, this was awkward. And wonderful.

Her breathing was slow and deep, so he was guessing she was still asleep, giving him plenty of opportunity to rearrange them out of this compromising position. The problem was, he didn't want to move. It just felt too damned good. She felt so warm and sweet in his arms. He liked this softer, vulnerable side. She was usually so capable and independent. Meaning, the instant she woke, he ran the very possible risk of getting an elbow jab to the ribs.

Despite the inevitable consequences, the hand cupping her breast seemed to take on a will of its own. His thumb grazed slowly back and forth, until he felt the peak of her breast tighten into a rigid point. Maggie made a soft mewing sound and tucked her behind more firmly against him.

He felt like a degenerate, taking advantage of her in her sleep. Of course, she'd wanted to stay, and he'd warned her their second day here that it had been a long time for him. Sleeping in the same bed, something like this had been bound to happen eventually. She'd had every opportunity to go back to her own room, so this couldn't really be construed as his fault. And he hadn't even opened his eyes, so technically he wasn't awake yet. She couldn't expect him to be responsible for his actions while he was asleep. Right?

Any other excuses you can dredge up, Pete?

He gave her breast a little squeeze. She sighed, wiggling her backside against him, and he struggled not to moan. He felt like a ticking bomb. A little more of her squirming just might be enough to set off an explosion.

He felt like a hormonally challenged kid. It was taking every ounce of willpower he possessed not to rub himself up against her. Even he had limits on how blatantly inappropriately he would behave.

Maggie let out a sigh and rolled in his arms until she faced him. She tucked her face against the crook of his neck and her hand landed on his bare backside. Her breath was hot on his throat, her breasts soft against his chest.

As if their position wasn't intimate enough before. This was downright torture. He had no choice but to wrap his arm around her.

Well, that wasn't exactly true. He had all kinds of choices, like rolling over to the other side of the bed. Or, since falling back to sleep at this point would be impossible, he could climb out of bed altogether and take a cold shower.

Instead he found his hands sliding down her back, until he cupped the swell of her behind. He was wide awake now. Without the guise of sleep to hide behind he felt even more guilty, more lecherous. That didn't stop him from stroking her behind, dipping his thumb under the edge of her panties. Then Maggie laid her hand over his and he froze.

Was she awake? And if so, why hadn't she slugged him? It seemed clear he deserved it.

Instead, she took his hand and guided it to the front of her panties. He was so astonished that for a minute he wasn't sure what to do. Well, he knew *what* to do—he could think of a couple of dozen things right off the top of his head—he just didn't know if he *should*. If she was asleep, then touching her would be wrong.

She'd been so adamant about keeping their relationship professional, there was no way she was anything but sound asleep.

There was one very simple solution. Give her a shake and wake her up. It was that or touch her, and risk having her wake right in the middle of…well, whatever they might be doing, and have her blast him for taking advantage of her.

So why wasn't he waking her?

Because deep down he wanted to believe she was awake and knew exactly what she was doing. He wanted to believe that not touching was just as damned hard for her as it was for him.

He held very still, waiting to see what she did. He would give her thirty seconds. If she didn't move by then, he would pull his hand away.

But she did move. She let out a little groan of protest and arched against his hand, as if to say come on, touch me. With an invitation like that, how could he *not* touch her?

Very lightly he rubbed her through her panties and she pushed herself against his fingers, muffling a moan against the crook of his neck. Her hand was back on his rear end, clutching and pulling him closer, her nails digging into his skin.

Okay, there was no way she could sleep through this. She had to be awake now, which meant he could stop rationalizing this and let nature take its course.

He slipped his hand under the edge of her panties, between her thighs, found her hot and slippery. She gasped and spread her legs.

She reached between them and wrapped her hand around his erection, and he nearly swallowed his tongue. As much as he would have liked to rip those skimpy panties off her and bury himself deep inside that wet heat, sexual petting was a far cry from making love. He'd abandoned the idea of casual sex back in med school.

But what they were doing now, this was…*exciting*. It made him feel sixteen again, when he'd touched a girl intimately for the first time. Only this time he wasn't fumbling his way through, hoping he was getting it right. He knew exactly what to do, where to touch, to give her pleasure. He cupped his free hand over her breast, pinching lightly through the fabric of her shirt, and her grip on him tightened, her pace quickened.

Aw, man, he was close. He didn't want to come first, but he could feel his control slipping.

Maggie's hips rocked back and forth, keeping time with his stroking fingers, then she moaned and arched against him, her body shaking with release. That was all it took to push him over the edge. Honestly, it was a miracle he lasted longer than thirty seconds. It was hot and fast and draining, as if all the tension, all the stress of the past five months had suddenly been lifted. He felt a little more like his old self.

And boy, did he need that.

Apparently, Maggie had, too. She burrowed against him and let a out a contented little sigh. Pete wrapped her in his arms and instantly felt himself slipping back to sleep.

Hours later, he finally pried his eyes open, squinting against the morning sun shining through the open window. He reached for Maggie, only to find himself alone, and had the bizarre feeling that it had all been a dream.

Maggie stood on the back porch, staring out at the water, sipping her coffee and trying to work up the will to feel guilty about what had happened last night.

How could something so wrong feel so *good?*

When she'd woken in the middle of the night with Pete curled around her, his hand on her breast, her body had screamed, oh baby! Her brain had done that short-circuit thing and instead of thinking oh, no, it had shouted a very clear oh, yes!

It had taken a good ten minutes of wiggling and shifting before he began to stir, but even then he hadn't gotten the hint. She would have thought turning in his arms and grabbing his butt would have done the trick, but still he'd faltered. Though she'd never considered herself the aggressive type when it came to sex, the guy just couldn't take a hint. She'd had no choice but to take matters into her own hands.

Literally.

When she thought about the way she'd taken his hand and put it between her legs, her cheeks burned with embarrassment. She burned with something else, too—sexual awareness. She felt it in her fingers and her toes and in the tips of her hair. She felt *alive,* in a way she never had before.

She also felt scared. She was setting herself up to be hurt again. Even if Pete didn't mean to or want to hurt her, it was inevitable. Though sometimes he seemed to genuinely care for her, when he got back home, back to his regular life, back to his old friends, he would feel differently.

"Good morning."

At the sound of Pete's voice Maggie's heart took a dive for her toes. She sucked in a deep breath and turned to him. He stood in the doorway, dressed in a pair of low-slung cut-off shorts and nothing else, his hair still rumpled from sleep. She would never be able to look at him again without remembering the way his body had felt pressed up against her, the way his fingers had teased her into ecstasy.

And while one part of her wanted to throw herself into his

arms, she knew that what had happened last night could never be repeated. No matter how badly she wanted it. Because it wouldn't last. One more good blow to her battered pride and she might never eat again.

"Morning, doc," she said, and turned back toward the water. She heard Pete sigh.

"Is that the way it's going to be?"

"What do you mean?" she asked, even though she knew *exactly* what he meant.

"We're just going to pretend that last night never happened?"

She closed her eyes. "I don't know about you, but I'd rather skip the we-shouldn't-have-let-that-happen speech."

He walked over and leaned on the rail beside her, gazing out at the water. Even at this early hour boats dotted the lake and gulls swooped down to scavenge off the beach. "Yeah, I guess I could live without that, too."

She only wished she could pretend it hadn't happened. She wished she could forget the way his skin had smelled musky from sleep, or how hot and hard he'd felt in her hand. His fingers had worked so skillfully and he knew exactly how to touch her until she completely lost herself. The memory was so fresh in her mind, so vivid, it was making her dizzy.

She glanced over at him and saw that his brow had tucked into a frown. He looked almost…hurt.

Maybe he thought she hadn't enjoyed herself. Maybe he thought he'd done something wrong. She didn't want him to feel bad or, even worse, feel as if he'd disappointed her. That couldn't be farther from the truth.

"Don't get me wrong," she said. "I had a good time."

He nodded. "So did I."

"It's just that things could get…awkward." She turned to look at him. "Things aren't going to be awkward now, are they?"

He shook his head.

"It was just an impulse thing, you know? A fleeting…" she waved her hands, searching for the right word. *"Whatever."*

A smile quirked up the corner of his mouth. "For someone who doesn't want to have the morning-after talk, you're having a hard time dropping it."

"You're right, I'm sorry. I just…" She sighed. "I guess I don't want you to feel guilty, as if you did something wrong. I mean, I started it, so it's completely my own fault."

He only stared at her, one brow lifted, as though maybe he wasn't certain of the exact chain of events, and she felt compelled to explain.

"If I hadn't been, you know, wiggling around, then you wouldn't have gotten, you know—"

He flattened one large hand very gently over her mouth. "I was there, I don't need a play-by-play of the action. All that will do is land us back in bed together, where you insist we shouldn't be. You don't need to beat yourself up over this, okay?"

She nodded, wondering what he would do if she bit him—or licked his palm—then decided that wouldn't be wise.

"Look," he said. "I was raised not to talk about my feelings, so this isn't exactly easy for me to say, but I really care about you, Maggie. You know that, don't you?"

She nodded. Though he didn't often say it, his actions spoke of his feelings for her. That didn't change the fact that his judgment was impaired. What he was feeling now would be very different from what he felt a month from now.

"We're both going through some heavy emotional stuff right now. As much as I would like to explore exactly where this relationship might go, I respect the fact that you're not ready for that. And as for last night, don't feel guilty. What happened was one-hundred-percent mutual. It was obviously something we both needed. It happened, and it's over, and we won't let it happen again. That *is* what you want, right?" He moved his hand so she could answer.

"Right," she said, her lips tingling from his touch. Which of course made her think about last night, and the other things he'd made tingle.

But he was right. And the way he'd explained it made sense. It probably *was* something they had both needed. Stress relief, or something like that. And now that they had gotten it out of their systems, not touching each other wouldn't be a problem.

She hoped.

Eleven

"Well, how is it?"

"One-oh-seven over seventy-five," Pete said and jotted the reading down on the chart he'd been keeping.

"So that's better, right?"

He pulled the blood pressure cuff from her arm and set it on the kitchen counter. "Yeah, it's better. Hop on the scale."

She looked with disdain at the scale sitting on the kitchen floor. In the past two weeks she'd grown to really hate that thing. What a god-awful way to start her day. "Can't we just skip it this one time?"

He crossed his arms and gave her his yeah-right look.

"Fine," she grumbled. She stepped over and lifted her foot—

"Shoes *off*," he said sternly, and she shot him the evil eye. "Don't look at me like that. You know the rules."

Mumbling under her breath, she kicked her tennis shoes

off, shut her eyes and stepped on the scale. She always kept her eyes closed. It was bad enough knowing she was gaining weight, she didn't want to see it, too.

On the bright side—and thank heavens there *was* a bright side to this—some of the clothes that had begun to feel a little loose were fitting again. She didn't get dizzy every time she stood up either, and she had more energy. She'd also had her first normal period in months.

"You've gained another pound." He marked that down on the chart as well. "Only three more to go."

"Does that mean I can start exercising again?" she asked.

"Don't push your luck. Besides, we've been walking. That's exercise."

Though it was nowhere close to the vigorous exercise she was used to, she had to admit the nightly walks they'd gotten into the habit of taking together—on the beach or through the woods or sometimes just down the dirt road—had become her favorite part of the day. It was a chance to relax and unwind and talk about everything or nothing in particular. Sometimes they didn't talk at all, they just walked side by side, quietly enjoying the evening.

One evening a few days ago, Pete had taken her hand to help her over a log that had fallen across the path, and he hadn't let go. He just kept walking, his fingers twined through hers, as if it were nothing out of the ordinary. She'd spent the next half hour debating; should she pull away, or just go with it and see what he did? Something about walking with Pete like that just felt so…natural. And every night since then, he'd automatically taken her hand when they left the cottage.

Besides, to worry about something as trivial as holding

hands seemed silly considering Pete had woken with bad dreams six times in the last two weeks—the last three nights in a row—and she'd wound up sleeping with him. And while nothing overtly sexual had occurred, Pete was a cuddler. He didn't seem content to sleep in the same bed unless he was lying all over her. And despite this becoming a regular thing for them, he still didn't wear pajamas. It hadn't escaped her attention that a certain part of his anatomy usually woke up well before he did.

She couldn't deny that she'd had the inclination to peek under the covers once or twice. Not that he would have known. Once he was out, the man slept like the dead. And it wasn't like she hadn't seen him naked before. The only problem was, she knew that once she looked, she would want to touch. She thought of how he'd shuddered when she'd wrapped her hand around him that night, how he'd felt long and hot and silky-smooth. The memory alone made her feel restless and needy.

So yeah, she definitely would want to do that again. And doing that could get her into a lot of trouble. So when she got the urge to peek, that was usually the point when she untangled herself from his arms and climbed out of bed.

"Three more pounds," Pete was saying, but she'd completely forgotten what they'd been talking about. She must have given him a totally blank look, because he waved a hand in front of her face and said, "Earth to Maggie."

She gave her head a little shake to clear it. "Sorry, what were you saying?"

"You asked if you could exercise and I said you have to gain three more pounds. Are you okay?"

"Fine." Just a mild case of sex on the brain.

"You sure? You really zoned out."

"I'm sure." And since she was feeling more than a little overheated, she opened the fridge, grabbed a bottle of water, and offered Pete one.

He took it and twisted the top off. "By the way, Jeremy called while you were in the shower."

"And…?"

"He wondered if I could fill in for another doctor and take on a couple of extra days at the clinic next week."

"How many?"

"It would be a full week."

She didn't doubt he was ready. She glanced over at the cane leaning in the corner by the door. The only time he used it now was when he was in an unfamiliar situation, or on uneven ground. And even then she didn't think he really needed it. He just wasn't yet ready to let go completely. He was still walking with a limp, but the truth was, that would probably never go away. She wasn't sure if he was ready to hear that, though. He still needed time to adjust—to heal. If not physically, then emotionally.

Working more was definitely a step in the right direction.

"So, what did you tell him?" she asked Pete.

He flashed her a grin. "I said I would have to check with my therapist first."

"Do you *want* to work extra days?"

He shrugged and took a swallow of his water. "If there's no one else to do it, I guess it couldn't hurt. I figured if you need the car you could drop me off and pick me up."

That was a big yes, if she'd ever heard one. "Well, even

though you won't admit it, you seem to really like volunteering, and God knows you've been a lot less cranky."

He raised an eyebrow at her. "I'm *cranky?*"

"And I can easily readjust your therapy schedule. I say go for it."

"You won't get bored here all by yourself?"

"Are you kidding? I can't wait to be rid of you."

He grinned, and his eyes locked on hers. He gave her that penetrating, soul-deep look that made her go all wishy-washy. She hated when he did that. It made her ache that much more for the things she knew she would never have. Though he didn't often come right out and say how he was feeling about her, he showed her in a million little ways.

She lowered her eyes. "I wish you wouldn't look at me like that."

"I just realized, I haven't thanked you for all you've done for me."

She lifted her shoulders in a casual shrug, eyes lowered to the floor. "No need to thank me. It's a job."

He tucked a finger under her chin and lifted, so she had to look at him. "You and I both know this has been more than a job."

She knew right then, by the look in his eyes, by the way his gaze wandered to her mouth, he was going to kiss her. She wanted to pull away, and she didn't want to. His head dipped lower and her lids slipped down. She felt his breath on her lips, his hand cupping her cheek, and her knees felt as if they might buckle out from under her. His lips brushed over hers and everything inside her went liquid. She found herself leaning into the kiss, into him, sliding her arms around his neck.

She felt his tongue teasing her lip, his teeth nipping lightly, and she went dizzy with desire.

"I want you, Maggie," he whispered against her lips.

But for how long? Though she was trying like hell to fight it, she couldn't deny she was falling in love with him. It was a lazy, easy kind of love that felt like a natural extension of herself—the logical next step in their relationship. But there was nothing logical about it. What would happen when summer was over and it was time to go home? How would he feel when he got back to his own life?

The ache in her heart became a persistent dull throb. She dropped her hands from around his neck and lowered her head. "I can't."

He sighed and rested his chin on the top of her head. "You want this as much as I do. Why do you keep fighting it?"

"You know why."

"We get along, we have fun together. We're sleeping together, for goodness' sake!"

"Not in the biblical sense."

"Why not? What can I do to prove to you that I have genuine feelings for you, Maggie? I'm probably one of the most emotionally stunted men you're ever going to meet, but if you tell me what it is I should say, what I should do, I swear I'll do it."

"If this about sex—"

He cupped her face in his hands. "You know damn well, this is not about sex. Why can't you trust this? Trust *me?*"

"This isn't a trust issue. I don't doubt that your feelings are genuine. For now, anyway. But you're going to feel differently when we go home."

"What if I don't?"

"What if you do?"

"But what if I *don't?*"

She closed her eyes and leaned her head against his chest. And Pete held her, because he didn't know what else to do. He felt like banging his head against the wall. He hated those bastards from her high school for making her feel unlovable, and her mother for making her feel inadequate. And she was wrong about one thing. This *was* a trust issue. And it wasn't him she didn't trust, it was her own convoluted feelings that were messing with her head.

Short of getting down on his knees and begging, he didn't know what to do or what to say to make her understand how deeply he cared for her. He might even love her. In fact, what he felt for Maggie went far beyond any form of love he'd felt before. It was complex and peaceful and exciting and *frustrating.* And the best thing that had ever happened to him. But he knew she wasn't ready to hear that. To tell her now would only drive her farther away. But eventually he would tell her. He would make her see what was so completely obvious to him— they were a perfect match. He would find the right time.

The only question was, when?

Pete reached up, watching his hand as it neared the elevator button, feeling an overwhelming sense of déjà vu. He'd done this before, he was sure of it. He heard the loud pops and spun around.

Then he knew, it was the shooting. It was happening all over again. Maybe this time it could be different. Maybe this time he could save her.

He ran past the screaming people, down the hall that seemed to stretch for miles, so far there seemed to be no end to it. He ran faster, feeling lighter than air, as if he were flying, still it stretched on. There was more gunfire, more screaming, but it sounded fuzzy and far away. Then he saw it, the junction of the hallway, where he would turn and find Rachel, and he already knew it was too late. Still, he couldn't stop, even though it meant facing the bullets that were sure to rip through him. He couldn't make himself turn around.

He finally rounded the corner, and there she was, lying in the hallway, soaked in her own blood.

No!

He knew what was next and he tried to stop it, tried to hit Rewind, but it was no use. His legs refused to stop moving. Then he felt it, the searing pain as the first slug hit his chest and stopped him dead in his tracks.

"Pete!"

The second slug threw him backward, then his knee exploded, sending him crashing to the floor.

"Pete, wake up!"

Pete gasped and surged up in bed, his breath coming in hard rasps, bile rising in his throat. "Damn it!"

Maggie knelt on the bed beside him, rubbing his shoulder. "It's okay."

No, it wasn't okay. Not at all. Instead of getting better, this was only getting worse.

He scrubbed both hands across his face, but he couldn't erase the vision of Rachel lying there. He could still feel the sting of the bullets. The pain. That would *never* go away.

"I am so damned sick of this," he said. "Is one night of uninterrupted sleep too much to ask for?"

As she had been every other night, Maggie was his voice of reason. "You're still healing. Give it time."

She was right. Though physically his wounds had healed, emotionally he was a still a wreck, and he didn't know how to fix that.

"I didn't save her," he said. "I failed Rachel."

"She died instantly, doc. There's no way you *could* have saved her."

Her words tore through him with the same ferocity as the bullets that had ripped through his chest. "If I hadn't taken my break, if I had been there with her—"

"You would *both* be dead."

He shook his head. "No. I could have gotten in front of her, I could have blocked it."

"And the second you went down, they would have shot her, too. It doesn't even matter, because it happened, and it's over, and all the guilt and remorse and what-ifs are not going to change the fact that she died and you lived."

The rational part of his brain knew that. He'd replayed that night a thousand different ways, and every time, as irrational as it was, he'd drawn the same conclusion; he should have been able to save her.

"It wasn't your fault, Pete."

"I know that."

"Then forgive yourself."

He shook his head. "I can't."

Maggie lay back on the pillow. "Come on, let's go to sleep."

He lay down and curled up beside her, his arm around her waist, his head resting on her shoulder. And as on every other night they'd spent together, she wrapped her arms around him and held him. He breathed in the scent of her skin, her hair, felt her stomach rise and fall as she breathed, needing her so badly he ached. She was in his arms, yet so damned far away.

"You're not sick of having to get up and come in here every night?" he asked.

She stroked the hair at the nape of his neck. "I know it's wrong, but I like sleeping with you."

It wasn't wrong. In fact, nothing had ever felt so right. All she had to do was say the word and he would have her out of that nightshirt. But unless she threw herself at him and said "take me," or gave him at least a vague sign that she wanted anything other than a platonic relationship, he would respect her wishes. Sleeping together—in the platonic sense—would have to be enough to sate this ever-growing need to be close to her. He was a patient man, so he would give her time. Time to see that what he felt for her had nothing to do with gratitude.

She was downright bossy at times, stubborn as a mule and annoyingly independent. She was also funny and sweet and understanding. And vulnerable. She was the first woman he'd felt he could really talk to. He *liked* talking to her. She knew more about him than Lizzy had ever known, or had ever *wanted* to know.

He and Lizzy had never been much for socializing with each other. They had always been busy doing other things—physically challenging activities that required little conversation. Now that he thought about it, he'd been engaged to a woman he barely knew. Not the way he knew Maggie. All those things he used to do, the activities he thought he would so miss after the shooting, had barely crossed his mind. Despite all the crap he was going through with the nightmares and the therapy, he couldn't remember a time when he'd been happier.

Beside him, Maggie's breathing had become slow and deep. She always fell asleep first. And as he had every night, he pressed a kiss to her temple, laid his head on her shoulder, and fell into a deep, dreamless sleep.

Twelve

"**H**ave you got a minute, Pete?" Jeremy stood in the door of the small, shabby little office the doctors at the clinic shared. It had been a long, busy five days, and now that Pete's Friday shift had ended, he was taking some time to catch up on his charts.

"Sure," he told Jeremy, setting his pen down. "What's up?"

Jeremy took a seat on the edge of the desk. "Just wondering how it went this week. It wasn't too much too soon?"

The truth was, it felt damned good to be practising medicine again. The hours he worked here were nowhere close to the long, grueling shifts in the ER. This was a cakewalk. In fact, the end of his shift seemed to come too soon, and he found himself stalling, taking one or two more patients before he quit for the day. "It's been good," he said.

"I noticed you're not using the cane anymore. The therapy is going well?"

"The truth is, I haven't had much time for therapy this week, but I've been trying to keep active. I swim in the mornings and Maggie and I go for walks every evening. She's talking about getting bikes this weekend, now that her weight is up."

"She's eating better?"

"Not as much as I'd like, but we're getting there."

"That's good. She's quite a girl."

Pete grinned. "She definitely has her moments."

"I'm having a barbecue a week from Saturday and I'd really like to have you and Maggie there. It'll mainly be staff from the hospital and their families. We're a pretty tight-knit group."

"I don't want to intrude…"

"No, it wouldn't be an intrusion. A lot of people are interested in meeting you."

"Why is that?"

"How do you like it up here, Pete?"

Pete sat back in his chair and folded his hands in his lap, wondering where exactly Jeremy was going with this. "I like it. Why do you ask?"

"Would you ever consider relocating here permanently?"

"I guess that all depends."

"The doctor you're filling in for this week has just been offered a private practice in Arizona. We're looking for a replacement."

"For the clinic?"

"The clinic and the ER. With your experience, you'd be a hell of an asset to the team. It wouldn't be the hectic pace you're used to in the city. The only gunshot wounds we get here are from hunting accidents, and stabbings are pretty rare. But Gaylord is a good place to live, a nice place to raise a family."

Pete's mind whirled with the possibility. Him and Maggie moving up to Gaylord permanently, starting a life together here.

He liked it.

The truth was, he didn't have much to go back to in Detroit, and he hadn't missed it since he'd been gone. But was he ready for that kind of commitment? Did he know for sure that Maggie was the woman he wanted to spend the rest of his life with? It stunned him how quickly the answer came. He didn't even have to give it a second thought.

Yes.

Without question, Maggie was the one. But how did she feel about him? What if she didn't want to live here? What if she didn't want the same things he did? They'd never really talked about it, not even casually.

"Think about it," Jeremy said, rising from the desk. "Come to the barbecue Saturday and meet everyone."

"Yeah," Pete said. He and Maggie were going to have to have a talk. And soon. "I'll definitely do that."

"That's four of a kind," Maggie said, adding up the dice. "Twenty-six points."

As she always did on nights that it rained, Maggie had raided the game closet. This time she'd chosen Yahtzee, and as usual she was creaming him.

He offered her the bowl of low-fat microwave popcorn. She hesitated, then took a handful without his insistence, popping a few kernels in her mouth, chewing slowly. Two weeks ago, she would never have considered an evening snack without a fair amount of persuasion from him. Though it was a slow, frustrating process, he was convinced she was well on her way to a new, healthy attitude.

"Your turn," she said, popping a few more kernels in her mouth.

"I don't know why I bother," Pete grumbled, but he scooped up the dice and rolled—two ones, two threes and a six. "What the hell am I supposed to do with this?"

Maggie peeked over at his score sheet. "You could try for a full house."

"I already crossed that off. All I need are fives and a long straight." He picked up the entire mess and rolled it over, and again got nothing he could use. "This is stupid."

"You keep saying that, yet here we are still playing."

She was right. Because despite the fact that he consistently lost, and Maggie had done her fair share of gloating, he was having fun. He wasn't scaling a mountain, or zipping over the snow on skis. He wasn't challenging himself physically, yet somehow, he was still having a good time.

Because he was with Maggie, and no matter what it was they did together, even if he was just sitting and watching her, how her eyes lit up when she smiled, or the way she bit her lip when she was concentrating, he couldn't escape this feeling of utter contentment.

But did she feel it, too?

"You have one more roll," she said.

He grabbed all the dice, rolled again, and got a big fat nothing.

"Wow, this really isn't your night," she said, gathering up the dice and rolling a long straight her first try.

When the game was over, Maggie had once again slaughtered him. She yawned, stretching like a feline, and looked at the clock above the sink in the kitchen. "No wonder I'm so tired. It's after eleven."

"I guess we should call it a night," he agreed, covering a yawn with the back of his hand. Although to him, going to bed just meant waking in an hour or two, drenched in sweat and gasping for breath. It meant images of blood and death. And the more he worked in the clinic, the worse the dreams escalated.

Sometimes he wondered if it would never end. But he wouldn't give in, wouldn't let it interfere with his life any longer. He was going to beat this thing.

"You want the bathroom first?" Maggie asked.

"You can have it," he said. "I'll clean up our mess."

"Okee-dokee."

Maggie headed for the bathroom and Pete put the game away, then gathered the dishes they had used for their soda and popcorn. By the time he'd washed and dried them, Maggie was ready for bed.

Pete used the bathroom next, brushing his teeth and, of course, picking up Maggie's discarded clothes from the floor and tossing them in the hamper. It had become a regular part of his routine—one he didn't mind so much anymore. It seemed a small price to pay considering all she'd done for him—forcing him to come here and face his demons. He was a better man because of her. A better person.

He finished up in the bathroom and walked to his room, thinking for a second as he got there that he'd made a wrong turn. Maggie sat in his bed, dressed in her nightshirt, reading a book.

"Hey," he said, not quite sure what to make of this. Either she'd had a serious change of heart, or he was hallucinating. Either way, she looked damned sexy sitting there, her legs curled under her, her face freshly scrubbed. She looked almost...wholesome.

She looked up and smiled, setting her book in her lap. "Hey. I guess you're wondering what I'm doing in your bed."

"I guess I am."

"I have a theory."

He leaned in the doorway and folded his arms over his chest. "Oh, yeah? A theory about what?"

"You never have nightmares when I'm with you, right?"

He thought about it and realized she was right. Once she climbed in his bed, he slept like a baby. "Not so far, no."

"Then I was thinking that if I sleep with you all night, maybe you won't have a nightmare. And let's face it, I'm probably going to wind up here eventually anyway."

"There is a definite logic to that."

"Unless you don't want me to."

Oh, no, he wanted her to. He just didn't know how much more of this he could take, how much longer they could sleep in the same bed, wrapped in each other's arms, before he went off the deep end. But she was right. Maybe sleeping together all night would keep the nightmares away. It was worth a shot at least. He would sell his soul for a night of uninterrupted sleep. "I think it's a good idea."

She set her book on the night stand and patted the bed beside her. "Hop in."

Outside, rain beat relentlessly against the side of the cottage, and cool, damp air lifted the curtains. Good sleeping weather.

He walked toward the bed, unfastening his shorts, and Maggie's eyes widened a fraction. "You might want to either turn out the light or close your eyes."

Her gaze strayed down to his crotch and lingered there. "I, um, don't suppose I could talk you into wearing pajamas to bed?"

"I don't own any."

"Oh. Boxers then?"

"I've been sleeping in the buff since college. I don't think I *could* sleep with boxers on."

"And you're not shy, are you?"

He grinned. "Nope. I see naked people in the ER every day. I kind of feel like a body is just a body."

Maggie reached over and turned out the light, plunging them into darkness, and he dropped his shorts and boxers to the floor.

"So," she asked. "If I was sitting here naked, I would just be a body to you?"

"No. If you were sitting here naked, we wouldn't be talking." He climbed in bed next to her, covering himself with the sheet. "You want to know what we *would* be doing?"

"No, I think I have a pretty good idea." She slipped under the sheet beside him, and they both lay down.

Maggie turned on her side to face him, and he did the same. As his eyes adjusted, he could barely make out the contour of her body beside him, the shadowy features of her face. Normally, after one of his dreams, he didn't hesitate to cuddle up next to her. Tonight he wasn't sure if he should. If that would be too...suggestive. Too forward.

As if she'd been reading his mind, she said, "This is weird."

"Yeah, it is."

"But nice, too. I like sleeping with you. Even though you're a *close* sleeper."

"Close sleeper?"

"You hog the bed, doc."

He smiled. She was right. The way he looked at it, if you were going to share a bed with someone, you might as well enjoy it. He liked to be close to Maggie. In bed was the only time she really let him get that close. Even then it wasn't nearly close enough.

"In my own defense," he said, "it's not a very big bed."

"No, it's not." She was quiet for a minute then asked, "You said that Lizzy was old-fashioned. How old-fashioned?"

"Where did that come from?"

"Just curious."

It kind of surprised him that it had taken her this long to ask about his ex. Not that it was one of his favorite subjects, but he didn't mind talking about it either. "If you're asking if we were sleeping together, yeah, we were. She just didn't spend the night. She still lived with her parents, and out of respect for them, I always drove her home. The odd thing is, I didn't mind. I didn't really think about it. Things just were the way they were."

"You don't miss her?"

"Honestly, no. At first I missed the idea of her, of the future. But we wouldn't have been happy together."

"Why not?"

"We weren't friends. We never talked. But that was as much my fault as hers. If I had it to do all over, things would be different."

If he had it to do all over, knowing what he knew now about love and friendship, they wouldn't last a week.

"Tell me about your parents."

Definitely *not* his favorite subject. He'd resigned himself a long time ago to the fact that they were never going to change, and he could live with that. If nothing else, he'd learned from them how *not* to raise a family. "They're very…rich."

She gave him a playful poke. "Tell me something I didn't already know. What are they like?"

"Cold," he said after a moment. "I suppose they loved me, but they never said it. Or *showed* it. I spent an awful lot of time trying not to be like them, but I guess some things you're just born with."

"You're not cold."

"No, but don't ask me to talk about my feelings."

"But you show your feelings in so many other ways. You can say you care for someone, but if you don't show it, the words don't mean much."

He reached up, stroked her cheek. "I care about you."

Maggie closed her eyes and sighed as Pete's fingers slipped through her hair. "I know you do, doc."

"You never use my name," he said, and he sounded sad.

"I like calling you *doc*. It's a term of endearment."

"I don't think so. I think it's just your way of distancing yourself from me."

She was about to argue until she realized that he was right. That was exactly why she didn't use his name. Calling him Pete felt so personal. So…*intimate.*

And lying here in the dark, touching and talking, wasn't intimate? Waking wrapped in each other's arms wasn't intimate? Not to mention that he was naked. You just didn't get much more intimate than that.

In every way possible this had passed friendship and drifted into relationship territory.

In every way except for sex.

"Maybe I'm still trying to look at this as a job. Trying to see you as my patient," she said. "But I guess it's not like that anymore, is it?"

"No, it isn't. Not for me."

"You know, when your parents called the hospital, and the director asked me to take your case, I almost didn't. I thought it might be a conflict of interest."

"How could it be a conflict of interest? We hardly knew each other."

"Yeah, but I kinda had these...*feelings.*"

"What kinds of feelings?"

"Before the shooting, I sort of...well..." She bit her lip, felt her cheeks burning. Why had she started this? "This is embarrassing."

"Don't be embarrassed. You sort of what?"

"I sort of had a crush on you."

Through the dark she could see him smile. "You did?"

At least he didn't laugh and point and call her a fool—even though that was exactly how she felt. And when she would have been better off keeping her mouth shut, she couldn't keep the entire, humiliating truth from spilling out all over the place.

"Sometimes I would find reasons to go down to the ER just to see you," she said.

"Really?"

Oh, great, Mags, now you sound like a stalker.

"Not all the time," she amended. "I just…you were always so upbeat and friendly and, you know…*gorgeous*. If I was having a bad day, seeing you would lift my spirits. Pretty pathetic, huh?"

"Not at all. You should have talked to me."

"You were engaged, I was engaged. And even if we hadn't been, I was fat. I wouldn't have approached someone like you in a million years."

"You should have," Pete said, slipping his fingers through her hair, twisting a curl around his finger. "We could have been friends."

"Maybe."

"*Maybe?*" he said, and he sounded hurt. "Maggie, do you have any idea what you mean to me? I don't even want to think about where I would be right now if you hadn't dragged me out here. You *saved* me."

A lump formed in her throat, and for some stupid reason tears stung the corners of her eyes. She felt…hollow. How could she be so close to someone and still feel so empty?

So *lonely?*

"It was my job to save you."

"Damn it, it's more than that and you know it," he said, his voice tight with frustration. "Why can't you tell me how you feel?"

Simple. Because she loved him. She loved him more than she'd ever loved another person, and she couldn't tell him. She was *afraid* to tell him. Because he might say he loved her, too, then she would have hope, when she already knew it was destined to end.

If anyone was emotionally repressed around here, it was her.

"Talk to me, Maggie."

"Doc—"

"No," he said. "Don't do that. Don't hide from me."

Tears welled in the corners of her eyes and slipped down her cheeks.

"I want to hear you say it," Pete said softly. He was close, his lips a whisper away. "Say my name."

Somehow she knew that if she did, everything would change. They would be treading on territory previously forbidden. She would be admitting her feelings.

The God's-honest truth was, she was tired of fighting it. Didn't she deserve a little happiness, even if it was short-lived? Maybe all these weeks they had been building up to this. Maybe it had been inevitable.

She trembled from the inside out, with fear and longing and anticipation. She wanted this so badly, but she was terrified of being hurt again. Sometimes she felt as if her entire life was just one long, painful experience she was destined to live over and over again.

Pete's fingers tangled in her hair, his breath tickled her lips. "Say it, Maggie. Say my name."

She knew if she did, he would kiss her. And this time it wouldn't end there.

She didn't *want* it to end.

"Pete," she whispered, and heard him sigh. His hands slipped through her hair, caressed her face, and she could swear he was trembling. She hadn't realized how badly he wanted this, too. He wanted *her.* Plain old, nothing-special Maggie.

But when she was with him, when he touched her this way, she *did* feel special.

"I want to hear you say it again," he said. His lips brushed tenderly over hers, as if he thought he might break her.

"Pete."

"Again," he whispered.

"Pete."

He captured her mouth, kissing her slow and deep and long, putting his heart and soul into it. Tears rolled in earnest down her cheeks. She wasn't sure why. Maybe she was happy, maybe sad—she just couldn't seem to pinpoint the exact emotion.

Pete cupped her face, felt that it was damp. He lifted himself up on one elbow. "Why are you crying?"

There was no way she could answer him, not without crying even harder. Instead she slipped her arms around his neck, pulled him to her and kissed him with all she was worth. She didn't want to talk anymore. She didn't even want to think. She just wanted to lose herself in his kiss.

And she wanted to feel him, the way she had that night, and more. There was so much of him to touch, she didn't want to miss an inch of it. She let her hands wander across his shoulders, down his back. His skin was smooth and warm, the muscles taut underneath. Her hands drifted lower, over his muscular backside.

Pete pulled away long enough to drag her nightshirt up over her head, then he stopped and just looked, as if the sight of her body amazed him.

"You're so beautiful," he breathed. Then he was touching her. Just like she'd always wanted him to—stroking her face, her throat, the valley between her breasts. She felt herself falling, tumbling deeper into ecstasy, dissolving in his arms.

He kissed her, deep and searching but unbelievably tender.

They were so close. In body and mind and spirit. She didn't know it was possible to be so close to someone. Not like this.

With his mouth still locked on her own, he slid her panties down and she kicked them off. Their legs twined, breath mingled. It was as if they just couldn't get close enough. Then he slipped a hand between her thighs, parting her, and she gasped at the intense sensation.

"You're so wet," he said, and if her skin hadn't already been on fire, she would have blushed. She felt wanton and heavy with desire. She wanted him to make love to her, *needed* him to.

He tormented her with long, torturously slow strokes and she arched against his hand. She felt feverishly restless, out of control. Her thighs parted, her legs came up to wrap around his waist. She'd never acted this way, never so aggressively, but if he wasn't inside her soon, she felt as if she would go out of her mind.

Pete hissed out a breath and looked down at her through the dark. "Tell me what you want," he said, his voice a hoarse whisper. "Say the words."

She caught his face between her hands. "Make love to me, Pete."

"Oh, Maggie." He entered her in one long, slow thrust, and her entire world shifted. In that second, everything she ever knew about making love was irreparably changed. She would never feel this again—this soul-deep connection. Not with anyone but Pete.

It was frightening and wonderful at the same time.

He withdrew, thrust again and her hips rocked upward, driving him even deeper inside her. She cried out as white-hot pleasure pulsed through her, all the way to the tips of her fingers and toes and the ends of her hair. She felt her mind going fuzzy, spiraling into oblivion. The air was thick with the scent of rain and the tantalizing perfume of sex. Their skin was slick with perspiration. She clung to Pete, to her senses, not wanting it to end. She wanted to feel just like this, be this close to him, but she was slipping, floating away…

Pete shuddered and groaned her name and her grip on reality slipped. The world exploded before her eyes, she splintered into a million pieces and she soared.

Thirteen

His heart jumping wildly in his chest, their bodies still linked, Pete watched Maggie as she went still and quiet beneath him.

Holy cow.

He didn't know what had just happened, but he felt as if everything he knew about his life, about himself as a man, had been knocked upside-down, turned inside-out and twisted all around. If he wasn't certain he loved Maggie before, he sure as hell knew now. Because the only thing he could think about as she lay peacefully in his arms, the only thing he wanted to do, was find a way to keep her there.

He knew if he told her he loved her, especially now, she wouldn't believe him. But, damn, he felt as though he would burst if he didn't say something soon.

Maggie's legs fell away from his hips, and she breathed a long, blissful sigh.

"Hey," he said, nudging her nose with his own. "I'm the guy. I'm the one who's supposed to roll over and go to sleep."

Her lips curled into a lazy smile and she gazed up at him, her eyes half-closed and glassy. She wrapped her arm around his neck and pulled him to her for a kiss. She tasted salty and sweet and delicious. The ringlets of hair around her face were moist with sweat, the skin between their bodies warm and slippery.

"We need a shower," he said.

Maggie groaned and tightened her grip on his neck. "I don't want to move. You feel too good."

"You don't mind being all sweaty?"

"Uh-uh." She slid her hands down his back and up again. "I like you sweaty."

This was a nice change from what he was used to. As physically active as he and Lizzy had been, when it came to sex, she didn't like to sweat. Now that he thought about it, there wasn't a whole hell of a lot about sex she did like. Just your basic missionary style. No frills, no excitement—no *fun*. He'd initiated oral sex a time or two only to be cut off at the pass and she wasn't really into trying new positions. In all the months they had been together, they'd never been as close, never as connected as he was with Maggie.

He wondered what exactly she might be willing to try…

He kissed her chin, her throat, the curve where her neck met her shoulder, and she made a soft mewling sound, rubbing herself against him.

Oh, man, did she feel good.

He cupped the weight of her breast in his hand, kissed and nipped at her slick skin, working his way lower, down the ladder of her ribs over her flat, toned stomach. Maggie moaned softly and stretched her body longer, didn't resist him when he pressed her thighs apart, when he lowered his head and tasted her. She gasped and dug her fingers into his hair, holding him in place, as if she thought he might stop.

Fat chance. He wouldn't stop until she was writhing in ecstasy, until he'd done things to her that in the past he'd only fantasized about.

And when they were both limp and sated and drained of energy, he was going to start all over again.

Pinkish light peeked through the curtains, and outside the window birds chirped. Maggie woke to find herself alone. She yawned and stretched and when she noticed the condition of the bed, a little shiver of satisfaction rippled through her. The top sheet lay sideways over her and tangled around her legs, and the fitted sheet had been pulled loose and lay rumpled beneath her, exposing three corners of the mattress.

Last night had been sensual and sweet and...*adventurous*. She hadn't known making love could be so much fun. Or so enthusiastic. Her tired, achy muscles protested as she rolled out of bed and stumbled into the bathroom. She brushed her teeth and tried to fix her hair, realizing that she would need a shower to tame the unruly curls. Giving up, she wrapped herself in the top sheet and ventured out of the bathroom in search of Pete.

She found him sitting on the deck steps, wearing only a faded pair of cut-off denim shorts, gazing at the water, sipping a cup of coffee. Dragonflies darted across the surface of the lake and spiderwebs glistened with dew. The air was thick with humidity and scented with moss and pine.

"Morning."

He turned to her and smiled. "Morning."

"You're up early."

"Couldn't sleep." He turned back toward the water and a tiny jolt of alarm passed through her. Something was wrong.

She sat behind him, sliding her hands over his chest, resting her chin on his shoulder. He set his coffee down and slipped his hands over her own, rested his head against her cheek. She loved touching him, being close to him.

"Bad dreams?" she asked.

"As a matter of fact no, I didn't have bad dreams at all last night. I guess your theory worked."

Though he didn't sound upset exactly, something in his voice set her on edge. And she knew, if she wanted to find out what was up, she would have to drag it out of him.

"What are you doing out here?" she asked.

"Thinking."

"About…?"

"My therapy. How in the past few weeks it's just sort of tapered off. I kept waiting for the real therapy to start, but what we've been doing, the walks and the swimming and the berry picking, getting me used to the disability, *that* was the therapy, wasn't it?" He looked back at her. "This is it. This is as good as it's going to get."

Her heart sank. She'd wondered how long it would take him to figure it out. "Pete—"

"It's okay." He gave her hands a squeeze. "It's not so bad, really. All the things I thought I would miss, I don't really miss them. I think…I think I've accepted it."

It was what she wanted—all she'd *ever* wanted for him— so why did she feel as if he'd just ripped out her heart?

Because now that he'd accepted it, the therapy was done, her job finished. It would be time for them to go home soon. Then everything would change. Even if they didn't want it to.

She laid her head on his shoulder and squeezed her eyes shut. It was over before it had really begun. But she didn't want it to end, *she* wasn't ready.

"I have to say something to you, Maggie, but I'm not quite sure how. I've been sitting here for half an hour going over it in my head, trying to find the words to explain it in a way you'll understand, that you'll believe, but I'm no good at this kind of thing. So I'm just going to say it, okay?"

Her heart sank low in her belly and her fingers felt numb and tingly. She was too afraid even to consider what he could possibly mean. But whatever it was, it didn't sound good.

Swallowing her fear, she nodded. "Okay."

"I love you, Maggie."

If he'd whacked her upside the head with a dead fish she wouldn't have been more surprised. And as much as she wanted to scream with happiness and thank God or Cupid or whoever for their divine intervention, it didn't change the fact that this was temporary.

His loving her was both horrible and wonderful and she just couldn't figure out which emotion she should let herself feel.

"I know you probably don't believe me," he said.

"No, I believe you." She believed that he thought he loved her, but that had no bearing on what he would be feeling six months from now.

"So why do you sound so miserable? Is it because you don't love me?"

She closed her eyes and pressed her forehead to his shoulder. "It's not that."

"Do you?" he asked, turning to face her. "Do you love me?"

"There are different kinds of love, doc." She cringed when she realized she'd called him doc again. It was her internal defense mechanism kicking in.

"We're back to that again?" He sighed and looked away. "So, what kind of love is it that I'm feeling? The pretend kind?"

"Pete—"

"It's a simple question, Maggie, do you love me or not?"

Tears burned her eyes. Why was he doing this to her? Couldn't he see that he was making her miserable? Did he enjoy torturing her? "We're going to go home, and you're going to get back to your regular life and this thing with me isn't going to seem so important anymore. It won't last, so it doesn't really matter what I feel."

Pete turned and lifted her into his lap, so her legs were wrapped around his waist. The sheet pulled to the side, leaving her completely exposed. Her breasts pressed against his chest and his denim shorts chafed her between her thighs.

"Yes or no, Maggie. I *need* to know." Pete took her face in his hands and forced her to look him in the eye. "If the answer is no, don't be afraid to say it."

He was tearing her apart. If she lied and told him no, she would hurt him. If she told him the truth, she would be hurting herself.

But she couldn't do it, she couldn't hurt Pete, even if that meant hanging her own heart out to be filleted and chopped to pieces.

"Maggie—"

"Yes! I do love you."

A slow smile curled the corners of his mouth and he pressed a very gentle kiss to her lips. She kissed him back— it was that or burst into tears. She didn't want to talk anymore. Didn't want to think.

His hands slid over her bare back, across her shoulders. When he kissed her so sweetly, touched her so tenderly, she could pretend they had a chance. She could make herself believe this would last. She could pretend this would all work out.

She felt herself melting, dissolving in his arms as the hands caressing her became more bold and the kiss went from sweet and sensual to hot and urgent.

Only when the sheet dropped away altogether, landing in a pile on the stairs below them, did it occur to her that they were outside and she was naked.

"Pete," she said breathlessly. "Someone might see."

He cupped her backside, fitting her more snugly against him. "No one will see."

He kissed her mouth, her throat, the tips of her breasts, and she was so dizzy with desire she didn't care if someone *did* see. All she wanted was for Pete to be inside her again. She needed him to be.

She rose up on her knees and unfastened his shorts.

Pete shoved them down. "Make love to me, Maggie."

Very slowly, so she could savor every sensation, every nuance, she lowered herself onto him until he was deep, deep inside her. They fit so perfectly together she wanted to cry.

"I love you," Pete whispered. He gathered her face in his hands, kissed her softly. "Tell me you love me, Maggie."

"I love you, Pete." It didn't hurt so much to say it anymore.

When they were like this, she could pretend everything was perfect.

Pete's hands wandered over her skin, touching her intimately, and she couldn't hold herself still any longer. Her body began moving—slowly at first, then faster, thrusting against him. Already she had that light, floaty, dizzy sensation in her head. Her body hummed and crackled with energy. She didn't want this to end, but at the same time she wanted to feel that completeness, that absolute connection she'd felt with no one but him.

"Oh, Maggie," Pete whispered, and at the sound of his voice, as his muscles coiled tight with release, she came undone.

Maggie sat in the shade on the deck in Jeremy's backyard, watching as the party buzzed around her, letting herself pretend, if only for a few hours, that she might someday have a life like this. Wives stood in clusters chatting about hospital gossip and children splashed in the enormous in-ground pool.

There was food everywhere. Chips and dip, vegetables and fruit, and everyone seemed to be snacking. She wondered if it would ever be that easy for her. If she would ever be able to look at food and not feel disdain. Not view it as the enemy. It was getting easier, but she didn't think she would ever lose the fear of being fat again. But it was getting easier to live with. Pete no longer had to force her to eat.

He'd been so patient with her—so understanding, yet firm. She didn't even want to think where she would be without him.

Across the yard—a rolling carpet of pristine emerald-green grass—Pete stood by the barbecue with Jeremy and several other doctors from the hospital. He looked tan and healthy and happy. He still walked with a pronounced limp—and always would—but to see him standing there, no one would guess the hell he'd been through.

Before her eyes, he'd become the confident, sociable man he was before the shooting. And despite their new intimate relationship and the countless times they'd made love in the past week, she couldn't shake the feeling they'd reached the beginning of the end.

He didn't need her anymore.

"Maggie, can I get you anything?"

Maggie looked up to find Mel, Jeremy's wife, standing beside her. Her long auburn hair was pulled back in a ponytail, her tank top pulled tight over the subtle bulge of her belly. Her face was free of makeup, giving her a fresh, natural look the other wives lacked. There was something about her, a sincerity that had made Maggie like her the instant they were introduced. She had also noticed that while Mel was friendly with the other women, she kept her distance. She was more of an observer than a participant. She reminded Maggie a lot of herself in that way. There was a look in her eyes, an insecurity Maggie could identify with. Given the chance, she could see her and Mel becoming friends.

Too bad they would never have the chance.

Maggie smiled up at her. "I'm good, thanks."

"Why don't you come inside and keep me company while I fix the potato salad?" Mel said.

"I'd love to." Maggie pushed herself out of the deck chair and followed Mel through the sliding-glass door into an enormous kitchen with every modern convenience known to man. Every room that she'd seen in the sprawling, Colonial-style home had been impeccably decorated down to the finest detail. Professionally decorated, Maggie was guessing, and everything looked brand-new. "You have a beautiful home."

Mel opened the fridge and pulled out a bowl of boiled potatoes, setting it on the island in the center of the room. "I told Jeremy I didn't need anything this big, but he insisted."

"I'll help you peel those," Maggie said.

Mel took two paring knives out and handed Maggie one. They each took a potato and started peeling. "Don't get me wrong, I really like the house. It's just not what I'm used to. When I met Jeremy I lived an apartment the size of my bedroom closet."

"How long have you been married?"

"Four months," she said, and laid a hand over her belly. "And since you're probably too polite to ask, I'm five months pregnant. Not planned, obviously. The consensus among the other wives is that I trapped Jeremy."

"Well, if you two love each other, I guess it doesn't matter what people think."

"That's what I keep telling Jeremy. It upsets him, though, that I haven't been accepted into the inner circle."

Maggie finished one potato and grabbed another. "Does it bother you?"

She shrugged. "For Jeremy's sake, I guess it would be okay. And it's not that they're bad people. They're just not *my* kind of people, you know?"

Maggie nodded. "I know exactly what you mean."

She wondered, would Pete expect a wife who would blend into the social scene? Not one who would always be on the fringes of the conversation—on the outside, looking in. He definitely deserved better. She didn't like to use the term *generic,* but someone who better fit the mold of a proper doctor's wife. Like Lizzy would have been.

He'd said that if he had it to do over, he would have done things differently. Maybe that had been his subtle way of telling her, or subconsciously admitting to himself, that he wanted another chance with Lizzy.

"How long have you and Pete been together?" Mel asked.

"We're, um, not exactly together. He's my patient."

Mel grinned. "I've seen the way that man looks at you. Whether you think so or not, you guys are definitely together."

"It's complicated."

Mel laughed. "It usually is. That doesn't mean it won't all work out in the end."

Maggie didn't even want to think about everything she and Pete would have to work out if they were to make a relationship last. She wouldn't have a clue where to begin. They were just too different. And too much alike.

Yet she couldn't help imagining herself and Pete married, living in Gaylord, her belly round with his child someday. She imagined long walks holding hands and long nights making love. On the surface it sounded doable—conceivable even—until she reminded herself that his feelings for her were temporary.

"I know Jeremy thinks the world of Pete. He's really hoping he'll accept the offer."

"Offer?"

"The ER position at the hospital." When Mel saw the look on Maggie's face, her hand stilled on the potato she'd been peeling. "Uh-oh, why do I get the feeling I just let the proverbial cat out of the bag?"

"It's okay," Maggie said, swallowing back a world of hurt and rejection. "I'm sure he was waiting until he made a decision to tell me."

Pete was getting on with his life, making plans for the future. It was a good thing. She was happy for him—even though on the inside, she was shattering.

"I'm sorry, Maggie, I just assumed you knew."

"It's okay." Maggie forced a smile. "I hope he takes it."

"Maybe he'll ask you to stay here with him."

Maggie gave a vague nod. If Pete had any intention of asking her to stay, he would surely have brought it up by now. But that was okay.

If he didn't ask her, it would save her the torture of having to tell him no.

Fourteen

"**D**o you miss your job, Maggie?"

Maggie lay in Pete's arms in the dark, legs looped, bodies slick with perspiration. They'd barely returned from Jeremy and Mel's party before Pete had begun kissing and undressing her, leading her toward the bedroom they now shared. And she'd let him, even though she was aching inside, knowing their time was almost up. She knew what she'd been getting herself into, and here she was, right where she thought she'd be—preparing for the end.

"Yeah, I miss it."

"You really love your job." He voiced it as a statement, not a question, as if he were trying to rationalize its validity. She loved her job, therefore she should go home and get on with her life.

"Yeah, I love it."

"So did I. I didn't realize how much until I started volunteering. I didn't realize how much I'd missed it." He held her tightly against him. "I'm ready to move on now. I'm finally ready to get back to my life."

Why didn't he just say it was over? Why did he have to hint around like this?

Guilt. He was too nice a guy just to blurt it out. To hurt her. He would try to let her down easily.

He stroked his fingers up and down the length of her spine, giving her shivers. "I think...I think it's what Rachel would have wanted."

Maggie squeezed her eyes shut. "She would have wanted you to be happy."

"I just wish I could close my eyes and see her how she used to be. But every time I try, I still see her lying in that hallway. I still see the blood."

"It won't be that way forever," she said.

"I'll always feel that her dying was unfair. I see people die all the time. But never someone I was close to. I guess I didn't know how to deal with it, and that was hard to admit. Kind of like your feelings toward food."

She gave a rueful laugh. "It's definitely a love-hate relationship. I thought when I lost weight my life would be perfect, but it doesn't get any easier, does it? I thought I was in control, but it was an illusion. I'd never been more out of control in my life."

"And now?"

"I know that life is work. There's no easy answer to anything. The important thing is that I'm healthy. And it's okay if I'm not always in control."

"How does your mom feel now that you've lost weight?"

"She doesn't know about it. I haven't seen her since I started losing."

"Why not?"

"Because I don't want her to think that I did this for her—for her approval. I don't need that anymore and I don't want it. I did this for me."

"So, what? You're never going to see her again?"

"I will eventually. When I can deal with the fact that she's never going to change. When I'm ready to forgive her. I haven't reached that point yet. But like you said about your parents, at least they taught you how not to raise a family."

"You want that?" he asked.

"What?"

"A family."

I'd like one with you, she wanted to say. "Someday," she said instead.

He was quiet for a minute, then asked, "Are you okay, Maggie? You seem…sad."

No, she wasn't okay, she was miserable. She couldn't lie here like this with him and pretend everything was all right when it wasn't. And at the same time she wanted to hold on to their last bit of time together.

"I'm fine," she told Pete.

"Didn't you have fun today?"

"I had a lot of fun. I really liked Mel." So much that she was sorry they would never have the chance to know each other better, to be friends. "I'm just tired."

Sick and tired of being the one who was stiffed in the end,

the one who walked away with the booby prize—her own battered pride.

If he couldn't come right out and say it, if he couldn't make the first move and just end this, maybe she would just do it for him.

Tomorrow, she thought as she snuggled against the long, lean warmth of Pete's body. As he sighed and held her closer.

She would definitely say something tomorrow.

Pete pulled the SUV up to the cottage, cut the engine and hopped out, an uncharacteristic spring in his step. Everything was in place. Today was the day he and Maggie were going to have a talk.

She'd been acting a little weird this past week, ever since Jeremy's party. Much quieter than usual. He was hoping his news would be enough to pull her out of whatever funk she'd slipped into. He hoped it would be enough to make her see that he really did love her. He'd told her at least twenty times each day, still, he didn't think she believed him. She said actions spoke louder than words, so he hoped his actions today would do the trick.

He walked to the door and stepped inside, nearly tripping over the suitcases stacked there. Maggie's suitcases.

"What the hell?"

"I'm going home."

Pete looked up to see her standing in the bedroom doorway. Her eyes were red, as if she'd been crying. He had the sinking feeling something terrible had happened. A death in the family, maybe? "What's going on?"

"I can't do this anymore."

"You can't do what?"

"I can't stay here and pretend everything is okay. It's tearing me apart. I have to go."

She was leaving because of *him?* For a second he was speechless. "I thought everything *was* okay."

She gave him that look, the one that said he was full of it.

"Okay," he admitted, "you have seemed a little quiet this week. I should have asked what was wrong…"

"But you don't like to talk about feelings."

Boy, did she have him pegged. "So tell me what's wrong."

"Did you take the job?"

"The job? How did you know—"

"Did you take it?"

"Not yet."

"You should take it. You'll be happy here."

He knew, from the way she said *he* would be happy here, she wasn't including herself in the equation. "*We,* Maggie. I wouldn't be happy here without you."

She lowered her head, looked at the floor. "You say that now, doc."

Oh for cryin' out loud, was she going to start with the doc thing again?

"You should call Lizzy," she said.

Lizzy? Where the hell had that come from? "Maggie, what are you talking about?"

"You said if you had a chance to do it all over, you would do things differently. This is your chance."

He smacked himself in the forehead. "Oh my God, Maggie, I was speaking *hypothetically.* I didn't mean I wanted to get back together with her."

"But she'd be the perfect woman for you."

"Lizzy is cold and spoiled and self-centered. How would *that* be perfect for me?"

She didn't seem to know how to answer that one.

"Do you love me, Maggie?"

She lowered her head again. "Yes."

"And I love you. So wouldn't that make *you* the perfect woman for me?"

She looked so hopelessly confused, so genuinely conflicted, he had to smile. Why she continued to fight this, why she wouldn't believe he loved her, was a mystery to him.

He walked across the room to her, tucked his finger under her chin and lifted her face. "Why can't you let yourself believe that this is real?"

"Because good things like this don't happen to me."

The hopelessness in her eyes made his chest hurt. He pulled her into his arms and held her and she pressed her cheek to his shirt. "*Ever?* I mean, aren't you about due?"

She was quiet for several seconds, then said, "I guess I never thought about it like that."

"I know it's tough, Maggie, but you've got to have a little faith. You have to trust your feelings, and you have to trust me."

"I thought, because you didn't tell me about the job, you weren't going to ask me to stay."

"Is that why you've been so quiet this week? Because you thought I was going to tell you I was staying here and say *so long*? You actually thought I would do that to you?"

She looked up at him and nodded, her eyes filled with guilt.

"Next time, instead of making yourself miserable, why don't you just *ask* me? As my therapist you've never had a problem getting in my face and giving me what-for. It's one of the things I like most about you. Don't turn into a doormat now."

Anger sparked in her eyes, and he could see he'd gotten her hackles up. Well, good. He didn't like it when she got quiet and withdrawn. It just wasn't her. He liked her feisty

"Okay, fine," she snapped "So why *didn't* you tell me? Didn't you think I might have wanted to know?"

"You're right," he agreed, "I should have told you, and I'm sorry I didn't. I just wanted to make sure all the pieces were in place before I brought it up. I had certain criteria they had to meet before I would even consider taking the position."

"What kinds of criteria?"

"Well, you said you love what you do, so I thought you might be more likely to stay here with me if you had a job offer."

The feisty look drained from her face. "A job offer?"

"I told them if they wanted to hire me, they would have to hire you, too."

"You actually *said* that?"

"Yep."

She couldn't believe he would do that for her. That he would hinge his career on her. These were not the actions of a man who didn't have a pretty darned good idea of what he wanted. She couldn't stop the hope from welling up inside her and spilling out all over the place. She didn't want to stop it this time.

And since he didn't seem in any hurry to tell her what had happened, she couldn't help demanding, "So what did they say? Did they have an opening?"

"They said first they would have to check your references.

So I gave them the name of your boss at the hospital. I hope that was all right."

"And…"

"And they called her."

She gave him the evil eye. Now he was just dragging this out to torture her. Not that she didn't deserve it just a teensy bit. She'd done her share of torturing him, by not trusting him.

What had she been thinking?

"And?" she asked.

He grinned. "And if you want the job it's yours."

"Well, jeez," she said, giving him a playful shove. "Why didn't you tell me?"

"I was going to, then I came home to find your bags packed."

She folded her arms stubbornly over her chest. "And what about you? Did you take the job?"

"I start September first…but only on one condition. That you stay here with me."

"And if I don't?" Like that would ever happen. He would need a crowbar to get rid of her now.

"Then I'll have to follow your stubborn behind home and try to get my old job back. I'll follow you around for the rest of your life if I have to. If that's what it takes to show you this is *not* my imagination." He reached up, touched her cheek. "Whatever it takes."

He really truly loved her, and she was kicking herself soundly for not realizing it before. For not trusting him.

For not trusting herself. It was time she started.

"Can I ask you a question, Maggie?"

She nodded.

"Your patient, the one you were engaged to, did you love him?"

"I tried to make myself love him. I think…I think I was in love with the idea of pleasing my parents, and I knew how much they approved of him. But when it ended, when I got over feeling bad, and feeling guilty for disappointing them, I was relieved."

"He didn't make you happy?"

"I tried to pretend I was. But deep down I was just fooling myself."

"Do *I* make you happy?"

Tears gathered in her eyes. "Always."

"Even this past week, when you were so *un*happy?"

The tears threatened to spill down her cheeks. "That was me making myself miserable. You never did anything wrong."

"Do you believe that I love you? Real, honest-to-goodness-until-the-day-I-die love?"

She grinned. "Yeah, I do."

Pete sighed and pressed his forehead to hers. "Thank God."

"No kidding."

He cupped her face in his hands, kissed her. "If we're going to make this work, Maggie, we have to be able to talk to each other. If you have any concerns or any doubts you need to tell me."

"And if you're planning on making any life-altering decisions, you have to tell me."

"Well, I'm thinking about asking you to marry me. That would be pretty life-altering."

There was so much love, so much sincerity in his eyes, she

knew this couldn't be anything but one-hundred-percent genuine. "Ask me."

He grinned. "Will you marry me, Maggie?"

She got on her tippy toes and gave him a big, toe-curling kiss. "Absolutely."

That night, Pete had a dream.

He was back in the hospital in Detroit, standing by the elevator, but this time there was no gunfire, no screaming people. No fear.

He turned, and from around the corner there was a light. A light so radiant, so bright it should have hurt his eyes, but for some reason, it didn't. He walked toward it, more curious than he was apprehensive. It was as if it was pulling him, beckoning him closer. And as he rounded the corner he saw her.

Rachel.

She stood in the hallway, waiting for him. All around her the light glowed. It seemed to be coming from inside her, and at the same time it didn't. It was coming from everywhere and nowhere.

"Pete." She held out her hand. There was no blood, no horror, just her sweet, friendly smile.

He walked toward her, reached for her hand, and when they connected, her touch filled him with a deep sense of calm. That's when he knew: the nightmares, the bad memories—they were over. It was as if they had been erased from his mind. Every time he thought of Rachel now, he would see her like this. Full of radiance and life.

"Be happy," she said, and he felt her squeeze his hand.

He had so much he wanted to tell her, so much to say, but already she was fading.

"Be happy," she said again, but she sounded far away. He grasped her hand tighter and realized he was holding air. But that was all right, because he knew now that everything would be okay.

Then the last of the light faded and she was gone.

Pete opened his eyes.

The room was dark. Maggie slept soundly beside him, her breathing slow and deep. They were alone, yet he had the eerie, almost surreal feeling they weren't.

It had been a dream. Right?

Then he realized, it didn't really matter. The message had been clear. It was time to get on with his life.

He loved Maggie, and she loved him. Being happy and happy with her, that was the thing he definitely planned to do.

* * * * *

Silhouette Desire

Heidi Betts

and Silhouette Desire
present

Seven-Year Seduction
(SD #1709)

Available this February

For years Beth Curtis struggled to seduce her childhood crush, Connor Riordan...until, one night, she finally succeeded. The consequences of that single passionate night ended their friendship and broke Beth's heart.

Now, seven years later, the tables are turned and it's Connor who wants to seduce Beth....

COMING NEXT MONTH

#1705 TAKING CARE OF BUSINESS—Brenda Jackson
The Elliotts
How far will an Elliott heir go to convince a working-class woman that passion is color-blind?

#1706 TEMPT ME—Caroline Cross
Men of Steele
He is the hunter. She is his prey. And he's out to catch her at any cost.

#1707 REUNION OF REVENGE—Kathie DeNosky
The Illegitimate Heirs
Once run off the ranch, this millionaire now owns it...along with the woman who was nearly his undoing.

**#1708 HIS WEDDING-NIGHT WAGER—
Katherine Garbera**
What Happens in Vegas...
She left him standing at the altar. Now this jilted groom is hell-bent on having his revenge...and a wedding night!

#1709 SEVEN-YEAR SEDUCTION—Heidi Betts
Would one week together be enough to satisfy a seduction seven years in the making?

#1710 SURROGATE AND WIFE—Emily McKay
She was only supposed to have the baby...not *marry* the father of her surrogate child.

SDCNM0106